THE GOOD DISHES

The Good Dishes

Short Stories

by

MARY ANN PRESMAN

Adelaide Books
New York / Lisbon
2019

THE GOOD DISHES
Short stories
By Mary Ann Presman

Published by Adelaide Books, New York / Lisbon
adelaidebooks.org

Editor-in-Chief
Stevan V. Nikolic

For any information, please address Adelaide Books
at info@adelaidebooks.org
or write to:
Adelaide Books
244 Fifth Ave. Suite D27
New York, NY, 10001

ISBN-10: 1-949180-84-0
ISBN-13: 978-1-949180-84-8

Printed in the United States of America

For Margaret Park who has nurtured and guided the writers at The Fountains in Tucson; and for Peggy Stortz, fearless and generous leader of the Ex Libris Writers in Galena, Illinois.

Contents

The Good Dishes

Back in our grandparents' day
they were chosen as wedding gifts—

Pretty plates rimmed in gold
or painted with flowers,
delicate matching teacups and saucers

brought out for company dinners, birthdays,
Thanksgiving and Christmas.

But packed away now, or donated to Goodwill,
these good dishes do not do well
in microwaves and dishwashers.

Garage Sale

Crystal felt she was sorting through the chapters of her life as she hauled stuff to the porch for her garage sale. Was it still a "garage sale" if you held it on the porch? She was lucky to have a porch—one of the reasons she rented this first floor space in Mrs. Larkin's dilapidated old house. That, and the rent was reasonable.

All of Benton Square was unearthing their treasures this weekend; it was a sale the rest of the city marked on their calendars. In this older mixed neighborhood, you could find everything from genuine antiques to baby clothes, scads of books and more than a few old bicycles, many abandoned treadmills and racks of clothing in now-too-small sizes. The Benton Square Garage Sale was always held the first weekend in May to coincide with the annual rite of spring cleaning.

Crystal was not nearly so organized as to subscribe to any ritual of spring cleaning. And it wasn't that she had lots to get rid of—but she was low on cash and hoped this would be a way to make a few bucks.

The house afforded her two storage spaces, some shelves in a corner of the basement, and—for the more precious things—a large pantry at the back of her kitchen. She began her quest for candidates in the basement; if they weren't precious enough to be stored upstairs, wouldn't it seem they were likely items for the sale? Here was a box of Christmas lights used for stringing from the eaves—that one Christmas when she and Chuck, her ex, were imitating normal people as best they could. Disc jockeys weren't, by and large, normal people—what had she expected?

Also, a whole box of flower vases. From the days when she was being courted by Oskar, who worked at a greenhouse and sent her flowers once a week. They were the standard clear glass variety, but maybe someone was planning a big party and would want a boxful of vases. Definitely garage sale material.

An unwieldy cinched green plastic garbage bag contained white tennis shirts and shorts, even a tennis dress. She could still wear them, but she never played tennis at that club anymore. She could wear anything she wanted at the public courts that were within walking distance.

This box of old LPs really shouldn't be stored in the basement, although she had never noticed a water problem. When the radio station cleaned out all its LPs, she lugged them home by the boxful. All the music is on satellite or computer now. She didn't even have a turntable anymore, why was she hanging on to these 33s? Would they sell? Does anybody still have a record player? Crystal pulled out the first album in the box, curious to see what it might be. Captain and Tennille, with their goofy-looking dogs and proclaiming "Love Will Keep Us Together." Well, it did—for a while. Longer than it had worked for her.

Crystal was about to begin poking around in the pantry when Denise arrived, Ms. Enthusiasm herself.

"You could plug in that string of Christmas lights and hang them across the front of the porch," Denise suggested.

"That'll draw attention to your sale, even to people just walking by on the sidewalk."

"Will little twinkle lights show up that much in the day-time?" wondered Crystal aloud.

"Of course they will! There you go, being negative again." Denise began pulling at the tangle of lights with her plump fingers. "Do you want me to help, or don't you?"

Good question, thought Crystal.

"If I were you, I'd put a few of those albums outside the box—on display like—so people are tempted to look inside," Denise continued.

Denise was in her element—organizing stuff was her strong suit. Her own house, a few blocks away on one of the better streets, was clear of clutter. "If I don't use it or wear it over the space of twelve months—out it goes!" And by god, she stuck to it. Crystal surmised Denise's husband, Martin, made sure he stayed useful. He put in long hours at the office, provided well for his family, and spent his weekends working outside when the weather was good, in the basement when it wasn't.

"Gosh! These are a mess!" Denise plopped down on the porch swing, sending it swaying. The hooks in the porch ceiling strained noisily, but the swing held. Unperturbed, she set about systematically straightening out what Crystal guessed was at least three strings of lights.

No one ever took them for sisters. Well, they weren't really full sisters, they were half-sisters—same mother, different fathers. Crystal took after their mother—dark-haired, tallish, thin and more-or-less indecisive. Denise, on the other hand, inherited not only a sturdy blond physical presence, but her father's take-charge capabilities. It was his resolve that had saved their mother's life, Crystal realized, but it had made her rebel as an adolescent. New father, new rules, no longer the sole focus of her mother's attention. She'd made a mess of her teenage years—and on into her twenties. Which was what gave Denise, ten years her junior, the prerogative to boss her around.

"Is this all the stuff you have?" Denise asked.

"No, I haven't even dug into the pantry yet. But the sale doesn't start til nine tomorrow. I can get more stuff out in the morning." Crystal perched on the porch railing and thought how good a cold beer would taste.

"You should have it all out here before it gets dark so you can see how best to arrange things. And you'll want to put price tags on all of it. Do you have something to use for price tags?"

"Price tags?" The thought hadn't even occurred to Crystal. Criminy.

"You *could* do those in the morning," Denise allowed. "But all the more reason to get everything out here now. You want me to help?" She made as if to get up from the swing, but Crystal moved quickly to put a hand on her shoulder.

"No. That's all right. I can do it. You've taken on quite a job there." Crystal headed for the door.

"Were you just going to sell these all tangled up?"

"I guess." She let the screen door bang behind her and headed for the pantry.

Crystal eyed the couple of boxes in the far corner of the pantry—the safest place to store her mother's good china. Better not haul those out now. Instead, she reached for a stack of board games—*Sorry* and *Clue* and *Yahtzee* and the like. Nobody played board games anymore, they were all hypnotized by the screens of their smart phones, playing *Angry Birds*. She set the games on the kitchen table and removed the top one, setting it aside. Crystal wasn't ready to give up on a face-to-face game of *Scrabble*.

She picked up the remaining stack and headed for the porch, pushing the screen door open with her slim hip.

"Oh, those are good!" exclaimed Denise. "Perfect garage sale material. Here, put them over on the swing where people can see them right away." She stood, the tangle of Christmas lights miraculously straightened out and fastened in reasonable loops, as if they were a cowpuncher's rope.

Crystal waited for the swing to stop swaying and then set the games down. Denise put the lights on the table and scooched the stack of games sideways and over to one end of the swing. "That way you'll have room for more stuff here," she advised.

"Right," acknowledged Crystal.

"I'm really sorry I won't be able to help you tomorrow, but the Art Guild Brunch is a big fundraiser and it just wouldn't do for me to miss it—being the brunch chair and all."

"Oh, don't worry. I'll make out. Too bad they're scheduled on the same day, though. You probably didn't realize that when you set the date."

"Well, you have to admit, it's not the same crowd," Denise pointed out. "And I suspect there won't be a swarm of people all at once, although I haven't been to a garage gale in years so I'm no expert."

"I wasn't here last year, so I don't know," said Crystal. "I mean, I was living here, but I wasn't in town for Benton Square's Garage Sale."

"Was that the weekend you went off with that florist person?"

"No, I think I was in Kalamazoo interviewing for a job at a radio station."

"Wasn't he gay?"

"You mean, because he worked at a greenhouse?"

"Well...?" Denise sort of fluttered her hand in a questioning gesture.

"Oskar definitely is not gay."

"Really?" Denise wanted more information, but Crystal was not about to give it to her.

"What do you think I should use for pricetags?" Crystal looked around as if some logical material would reveal itself.

"They sell them in little packages—little tags with strings in them and everything."

"Where?"

"Oh, like at Michael's or Office Depot. Places like that."

"Really?"

"Really. Why don't I just run out and get some for you?"

"Do you have time?"

"Sure. It'll just take a half-hour or so—I know right where to go. It'd take you forever." Denise smiled indulgently. "But then I'll have to drop them off and be on my way. Can you figure out the prices for yourself?"

"I'll manage," Crystal said.

"Okay then, I'm off." Denise grabbed her car keys and purse and pushed open the screen door.

Well, that worked.

Crystal returned to the pantry for more garage sale candidates. How had she managed to accumulate so many plastic containers? They were stacked—sort of—in a corner closest to the pantry entrance, ready to be snatched up and filled with—what? Leftover mostaccioli? Her landlady's applesauce? A collection of rubber bands and twist-ties? Hopes and dreams?

She wondered if anyone would actually buy them. Perhaps some earnest recycler might. She dumped them in a brown paper bag without bothering to match lids to containers and took them to the porch. Playing matchmaker would be a good project for Denise if she returned with any extra minutes to grant to Crystal's Garage Sale Project. Denise was best kept busy.

More staring at stuff on the pantry shelves. She definitely did not want to take her mother's dishes out there until Denise had come and gone for the last time. How about this bread maker? Whoops! She remembered in the nick of time that Denise and Martin had given it to her for Christmas a few years back. She'd used it a couple of times while married to Chuck but not since. Crystal in the kitchen was like Mr. T in a "White Gloves and Party Manners" class. She'd add the bread baker to the sale items first thing in the morning, when Denise would be busy going over her plan of attack for the Artists Guild Brunch.

A slam of the porch door announced Denise's return. "Here they are," she called out, as Crystal went to greet her. "Just where I thought they'd be...at Office Depot." Denise waved a plastic bag in the air and handed it to her sister.

"Thanks," Crystal said. She peered inside and pulled out the tags. "These are perfect." She smiled at Denise. "I never knew such a thing existed."

"Right...they're just what you need. Glad I could help." Denise looked around. "Is this all the stuff you have?"

"Oh, I'm still deciding on what can go and what I want to keep."

"If I had more time, I could help you with that...but I don't. Sorry."

"It's okay. I just have to put on my Practical Person hat and get to it," Crystal said.

"It's not easy, I know. Some things are difficult to part with." Denise smiled. "Well, gotta run. Good luck with all of this tomorrow." She gave Crystal a hug. "It's supposed to be a nice day, so that should promote traffic."

"Right. And good luck with your brunch thingy." Crystal followed Denise to the porch door. "And thanks again for all your help," she said, as Denise descended the porch steps.

Crystal turned back to the porch with the price tags in her hand. She looked at the box of vases. She certainly wasn't going to put an individual price tag on each vase. She went into the kitchen and found a black marker in the "everything" drawer. **ANY VASE – 50 cents** she wrote on the side of the box. **LP's – 3 for $1**, she printed in large letters on that box. She recognized the apostrophe as a grammatical error, but it looked better that way. And made up for all the apostrophes left out in crossword puzzles.

What would she use the price tags for? Back to the pantry. It was probably safe to take the Bread Maker out now, but she had no idea what price to put on it. She didn't even know what they cost new. Have to look that up on EBay.

And then there were her mother's good dishes.

Crystal was standing in the kitchen with her first cup of coffee the next morning when she thought she heard a thump on the porch. She went over and peered through the closed storm door. She moved sideways so she could see outside. Somebody was standing there, peering into the porch. She glanced at the clock—7:37 a.m. She looked down to be sure she was fully clothed, then opened the storm door.

"The garage sale doesn't start until nine o'clock," she said, still behind the kitchen screen door.

The man lowered the hand he used to shade his eyes and smiled cheerfully at Crystal.

"Oh, I know. I thought I'd take a look-see before I went for breakfast so I know where to come first."

She looked him over carefully. "It's a little early to be peeking into people's porches."

"Oh, crap! I didn't scare you, did I?" He backed down a step. "I didn't even think about that."

"You're lucky I didn't have my six-shooter handy," Crystal said, grinning at the man's obvious embarrassment.

"Are you a good shot?"

"Darned if I know," she admitted. Crystal opened the door and stepped onto the porch. "Are you looking for something in particular?"

"Oh, I'm in the market for all kinds of stuff." He stepped back up to the top step, but remained on his side of the outside screen door and made no move to open it. "I'm just moving into an apartment kinda close by and I'm going to need furniture … lamps … pots and pans … kitchen utensils … that kind of thing."

"Well, you're in luck. You'll find all that and more at the Benton Square Garage Sale. Good timing on your part." She walked over and stood just this side of the door, wanting to get a better look at this prospective customer…new neighbor… whatever he was. "I can't let you in yet. They get pretty cranky about that."

"They?" the young man asked. Because she could see now that he was what Crystal would call young –about her age, really. Kind of an average-looking guy. No distinguishing tattoos or abnormalities that would make him stand out in a police lineup.

"The Benton Square Garage Sale Committee." Crystal lowered her voice an octave to become an imaginary committee person. "'If one person starts selling early, then people will expect others to do the same, and we lose all control over the hours of the sale.'" She smiled. "Can't have an out-of-control garage sale."

"Right. All heck is likely to break loose."

"And to be honest, I don't even have all my stuff out here yet. There'll be more when you come back at nine." Crystal waved vaguely at was on the porch.

"Do you have any kitchen things?"

"There are some dishes that aren't out here yet. And a bread-maker."

"I was really looking for pots and pans," he said.

"Are you going to eat your dinner right out of the pan?" Crystal asked.

He grinned. "Of course not. What do you take me for—some sort of barbarian? I'll have you know I'm a respectable human being. My mom raised me right." Almost as an after-thought he added, "My name is Ned Sullivan."

Crystal transferred her coffee mug to her left hand, pushed open the door with her foot—causing Ned to back down a step—and stuck out her hand to shake his. "I'm Crystal. Wel-come to the neighborhood, Ned. Be sure you come back at nine."

"Oh, I will." He smiled and backed down the steps to the sidewalk. "For sure…I'll be back."

At least he didn't do an Arnold Schwartzenegger imita-tion—Crystal had to give him points for that.

After her second cup of coffee, Crystal carried the bread-maker to the porch. Then the heavy carton containing her mother's good dishes. She had saved a prominent place on the table for these—they would be her high-ticket items. The bread-maker looked "like new" in its original box with col-orful photos on the side. She rummaged around in the kitchen drawers and found the instructions in with hotpads and dish-towels. As she tucked the little booklet in its box, she began to feel organized. Well, a little.

People were beginning to drive slowly up and down the street, eyeing the houses with bright yellow Benton Square Garage Sale signs in front. It was a few minutes before nine; she stood contemplating the box with the dishes. Should she sell them as a complete set or allow people—like Ned, who wouldn't need a service for twelve—to purchase just a few pieces? Maybe she'd play that by ear. Probably should take out a few plates and a cup and saucer so people can see what they look like. She lifted a plate out of its newspaper wrapping and turned it over. "Ballet Icing" she read the name of the pattern aloud. "Ohmigosh, I didn't realize it was Waterford." She turned it back over, studying the pretty white-on-white scroll that edged the rim of the plate. When had her mother received these dishes? Who would have spent that kind of money? They must have been part of a bridal registry...so many years ago.

"You can't seriously be thinking of selling Mother's dishes?"

Crystal nearly dropped the plate she was holding. She didn't hear Denise come up the porch steps—her arrival muffled by the general hub-bub now taking place up and down the block.

"Aren't you supposed to be at a brunch?" Crystal stuffed the plate back into the box.

"I thought I'd stop by to see if you needed any last-minute help." Denise stayed a few steps inside the porch door. She glanced at the bread-maker, then looked from the carton containing the dishes to Crystal. "Seriously. You're not putting Mother's dishes in your *garage sale,* are you?" She practically spit out the words.

Crystal looked at the evidence. "That's the plan," she admitted.

"Crystal, if you don't want those dishes, I'll be happy to take them off your hands." Denise stepped toward the table. "You could give them to me."

"I could, but I could also sell them in my garage sale." Crystal moved so she was between the table and Denise.

"Those dishes should stay in the family."

"They're just dishes, Denise. It's not like they're photograph albums, filled with loving memories. Can you even remember these being used?"

Crystal knew her mother had used these dishes only on rare occasions. She wasn't even sure she had used them after she married Denise's father. Perhaps they were an unpleasant reminder of her first marriage.

"But they belonged to *our* mother," Denise argued.

"And she gave them to *me*," Crystal pointed out. "Neither of us has ever used them."

"Because they've been sitting in a box in *your* pantry."

"That's because these dishes are mine…and I can do whatever I please with them."

"If you'd stick to a budget you wouldn't be so hard up that you'd need to sell your…*our*… mother's dishes in a garage sale."

"The fact remains," Crystal stood taller, chin in air, "it's my prerogative to do so."

Denise stood a moment, biting her lip, then without another word she whirled and pushed open the screen door—nearly knocking over the person who stood on the steps.

Sure enough, it was Ned Sullivan.

"Unhappy customer so early in the morning?" he asked.

"Unhappy sister," Crystal admitted. "Sorry she almost knocked you over."

"I'm not easy to knock over." Ned smiled at her. "But sisters—or brothers, for that matter—have a way of exerting a force that isn't always physical."

"Ohmigod. An early morning psychoanalysis." Crystal feigned distress with a melodramatic hand to her forehead.

"Okay, sorry. It's none of my business," Ned said, turning away to look around the porch. "Let's see what you have for sale here." He took a few steps from Crystal, paused, and pointed to the box of dishes. "I think I'll stay away from those. Not exactly uncouth bachelor material, anyway, are they? Can you even put them in a dishwasher?"

"Darned if I know," Crystal admitted. "Probably not. Otherwise I might have been using them myself."

"Are you a bachelor?" he asked. "I mean…"

"Unattached."

"Are you moving?"

"No, I'm just trying to clear a little of the clutter out of my life…and make a few bucks." Crystal glanced at the merchandise. "Probably this stuff would just be clutter to you, too. I think the Schmidts over on the corner are selling some actual furniture."

"Hey, I might need some Christmas lights." Ned held up the strings Denise had so carefully untangled. He looked at Crystal. "Are you trying to get rid of me?"

"No, no. Absolutely not." Why did this fluster her? "I was just trying to be helpful."

"Thank you for that." He touched the brim of his baseball cap.

"You're welcome…"

"Ned," he said. "Ned Sullivan."

"I remember your name." She felt herself blush.

"Really? Good." There was that disarming grin again. "And you're Crystal, right?"

"Me Crystal, you Ned." Uh-oh. Was that a step forward too quickly?

He smiled even more broadly and raised the lights in the air. "Crystal with the Christmas lights for sale."

"I think I'm going to get myself some coffee." Crystal headed for the kitchen door, then felt compelled to offer, "Do you want a cup?"

"I'd love one."

When she came back on the porch with two mugs of coffee, Ned was looking through the LPs.

"I forgot to ask if you need cream or sugar." She tentatively offered one of the mugs to him.

"This is good." Sipped, nodded appreciatively. "You have quite a collection of LPs here."

"Yeah, I used to work for a radio station."

"Really? Here in town?"

"No. In a previous life, in another town."

"Were you a disk jockey? You have a nice voice."

"No." She blushed again, godammit. "I was a copywriter… wrote the radio commercials."

"Ah! So do you have an unfinished novel in a drawer some-where?"

"Not really." You couldn't call what she had in the drawer an 'unfinished novel.' "I liked working in radio, but it's not the same anymore."

"So what do you do now?" Ned continued to look through the LPs while he gleaned information.

"I work at the library."

"That sounds good."

"It *is* good…though it doesn't pay much. I'm essentially part-time. I keep hoping my boss will decide to retire so I can be promoted to Director of Community Relations. But she's still going strong!"

"Pretty inconsiderate." Ned lifted his mug to hers in a toast, "To early retirement."

Their mugs clinked.

"So, in an effort to augment my income, I've stooped to the unimaginable low of putting my mother's dishes up for sale." Crystal looked to Ned for sympathy.

He hesitated. "And the person that deems this such a dastardly deed is your sister?"

"*Half*-sister."

"Same mother ... or same father?" Ned turned slightly away so as not to be questioning Crystal face-to-face.

"Mother." Crystal wasn't sure she liked where this was going. "It's not like I have any kids to pass the dishes on down to."

"Does your sister have kids?" He pulled an LP out of the box to scrutinize it.

"Two daughters." If she hadn't given this guy a cup of coffee he'd be gone by now. "If Denise really wants the dishes, she could have them. She could buy them in the garage sale like anybody else."

"True." Ned glanced at Crystal, then returned to his study of Bruce Springsteen's face on a well-worn album cover.

Crystal waited for his next pithy question. Why did she feel the need for his—or anyone's—approval? "I mean, she has all kinds of money. It wouldn't bust her precious budget to pay for the dishes." That sounded whiny, didn't it?

Ned pushed the LP back into the box and looked at her. "I've already said more than I should have."

"So you think I'm in the wrong here?"

"Look, they're your dishes, aren't they? If your mother gave them to you—then you're free to do whatever you want with them."

"Right. At least, I thought so."

Ned poked in the LP box again. "Here's something you might consider..." and then his gaze met hers. "What would your mother want?"

Oh, god. Of course. Crystal walked to the porch door and stared out at the sunlit and shade-dappled lawn. It was so obvious, so simple. Why hadn't she asked herself that question? Because she knew the answer, goddammit.

"Crystal?"

She turned back to Ned. "It is so embarrassing to have to admit that I never asked myself that question."

"Maybe. But understandable."

"You don't think I'm a horrible person?"

"Number one, you shouldn't care what I think. Number two, for what it's worth, I don't think you're a horrible person. If that's the worst thing you've ever done…"

"Where did you come from?" Crystal asked.

"Never mind that…look who's coming up the walk." Ned moved back behind the box of LPs.

It was Denise, in a very big hurry. She pounced up the steps and pulled a handful of bills out of her pocket. "I went to the ATM. I knew you'd want cash. Will eighty dollars cover it?"

"I've had a change of heart, Denise. Mom's dishes are not for sale." Crystal didn't back up from where she stood, so the two sisters were face to face, the porch door hung open. She waited while Denise attempted to compose herself and then resisted the temptation to further torment her. "They're yours."

Denise looked bewildered.

"Seriously." Crystal stepped to the table and began rewrapping the plate to put it back in the box. "I'll never use these dishes. You will. And then maybe your daughters will." She gave Denise a rueful smile. "Mom would have liked that."

Denise looked over at Ned in wonder. He raised his coffee cup to her.

"I know you have that brunch thing. Why don't I just pack them up and you can pick them up tomorrow?" suggested Crystal.

"Are you sure? You're *giving* them to me?" Denise made a halfhearted effort to offer Crystal the cash still in her hand.

"I'm sure. I promise I won't change my mind." She made a show of looking at her watch. "But you'd better get going."

"Right." Denise looked again at Ned. He grinned. "Thanks so very much," she said, hugging Crystal. Tears welled in her eyes as she turned and hurried down the steps, stuffing the cash back into her jacket pocket.

Crystal eyed Ned. "I think Mom sent you."

He shrugged. "Does that mean I already have Mom's approval?"

Hey! diddle, diddle,

The cat and the fiddle,
The cow jumped over the moon;
The little dog laughed
To see such sport,
And the dish ran away with the spoon.

Should the Dish Run Away With the Spoon?

I suspected my mother was turning over in her grave. Here was her supposedly respectable librarian daughter meeting the Trailways Bus from Durango, bearing one Zeke Gramercy, cowboy poet.

I didn't even know what Zeke looked like, but then he didn't know what I looked like either.

"Let's not trade photos," he said when we were first getting acquainted on *heartsafire.com.* "I don't think relationships should be based on physical appearance. Do you?" He had inserted one of those smiley-faced emojis after the word *appearance.* I took that to mean he's always smiling.

"How will I know which one is you?" I asked when he telephoned to tell me he had bought his ticket.

"I'll be the one in a cowboy hat."

My hometown's bus station is pretty sad—not really the kind of first impression one would want a visitor to have. This is, after all, Chillicothe, Illinois, not the much bigger and better known Chillicothe in Ohio. The low-slung grey cement block building contains rows of plastic folding chairs designed to discourage sleepovers, plus a wall of chancy vending machines.

But with any luck, Zeke would never see the inside of the building, just the concrete parking lot where buses pulled in. My stomach clenched as the bus arrived in a whoosh of nasty fumes. The hydraulic door eased open and Trailways passengers disembarked, some laden with bulging shopping bags, others claiming various forms of luggage from the baggage compartment.

And then he stood before me—not a John Wayne cowboy, more like Dustin Hoffman—dressed in clean but faded denim and grinning ear to ear. He was much shorter than I imagined. Zeke looked me in the eye, tipped his broad-brimmed Stetson and said, "Miss Karen Halek, I presume?" Then he stuck out his hand.

"And you're Zeke." I reached out my hand to shake his. "Welcome to Chillicothe."

"Thank you." He held my hand just a moment longer than a normal handshake required. "I'm delighted to actually make your acquaintance in person."

"Me too. I'm delighted, too. That we get to meet in person." God help me—where was any semblance of intelligent conversation? "Um, do you have any luggage to claim?"

"No, I'm all set," he said, indicating the small canvas bag in his left hand.

"Okay then. My car's over in the parking lot across the street."

Zeke touched my forearm. "What say we have some lunch and the beginnings of our get-acquainted conversation first? Is there a café near here?"

Uh-oh, he's having second thoughts already.

"That way, if you decide you aren't sure about having this cowboy under your roof, I can either find lodging elsewhere or hop the next bus home."

I wondered if he's done this before…hopped a Trailways bus to explore a relationship begun online? Maybe that's something I could ask over lunch.

"There's La Familia across the parking lot and down a block. If you like Mexican?"

"Perfect. Lead the way." Zeke swung his bag into his right hand and gently placed his left hand under my elbow as we stepped down off the curb. I tried to see downtown Chillicothe through a stranger's eyes: gentle mid-May sunshine cast the brown-brick storefronts in their best light, a few blocks of floundering commercial enterprise huddled along North Fourth Street, hoping the economic recovery wouldn't arrive too late for this Illinois River town.

I felt that Zeke was not looking so much at Chillicothe, but studying me.

I wore a new pair of flats that I hoped looked trendy; I had allowed myself to purchase them to go with a favorite old dress—green looks good on me. My shoes were too new to walk far in, I was glad when we settled into a booth at La Familia.

"This seems like a good place," Zeke removed his hat, revealing a thick head of salt-and-pepper hair and affording a better look into his friendly grey eyes. He put the Stetson on the seat beside him, then surveyed our surroundings, taking in the walls painted with scenes of burros, Mexican senoras, and children kicking a ball around. Twinkling colored lights festooned a fake saguaro in the corner—La Familia's year-round version of a Christmas tree. The unmistakable fragrance of sautéed onions and peppers hung unapologetically in the air.

Zeke glanced at the menu, then put it down. "I thought you told me you were forty-one?"

"I am. Forty-one and then some—my birthday's in August."

"I know that part. August 27. But maybe I don't know what forty-one looks like anymore, 'cause you look… maybe… thirty-three, thirty-four."

We had established online that Zeke is fifty-nine. He looked every bit of that in the weathered way I imagined cowboys should look.

"Do you want to see my driver's license?" I asked.

"No, no. See, that's a compliment. I'm not questioning your veracity—only making an observation. Take it as a compliment."

"Okay." So now I wondered if he really thought I looked younger or if he was just handing out compliments. I'm not what you'd call homely, but I'm not a stunning beauty either. What did he see as he carefully studied me? A tall-ish brown-haired woman a little on the skinny side. "You're quite the smooth talker."

"Is that good or bad? What do you mean, 'smooth talker'?"

I hesitated. "'Veracity.' Not too many cowboys come up with 'veracity.'"

"How many cowboys do you know?"

"You're the only one," I admitted. I liked his voice—confident without being a know-it-all. He seemed so at ease—he *must* have done this before.

"Let's hope I'll give the cowboy classification a good name." He winked at me. "That's what you librarians do, isn't it? 'Classify' things?"

"Well, kind of. They're pretty much classified when they arrive. Fiction, non-fiction."

"What do you think this is?"

"This?" I wasn't sure whether he meant La Familia or Chillicothe or…

"Our meeting. Taking a chance. Is this for real?"

"I guess we'll find out." A waitress came with water and menus. Thankfully, she was not someone I recognized—otherwise, I would have felt the need to introduce her to Zeke. That's the kind of small town Chillicothe is.

Zeke glanced at the menu. "Are you in a rush? Do you have to get back to work?"

"No, I switched with Eileen so I have the day off." Eileen Whitcliff had been only too happy to be even a small part of this wild and crazy scenario. She spent a lot of time in the romance novel stacks.

"Hey, that's great." He settled back in the booth, moved his shoulders around. "Maybe we can take a little walk around town after lunch. I'm kind of stiff from that long bus ride."

"I think we should take your bag back to the house first; then we can walk." This was the arrangement we made online. I have a big old house with lots of rooms—it's the house I grew up in and where I've always lived. No sense in Zeke spending money to stay at the Super 8. It's not something I've done before and I admit it may not be the smartest move I've ever made, but hey, I'm a big girl. "After you unpack you'll know if there's anything you've forgotten. Anything you need to purchase at the drugstore or anywhere."

I felt the flush in my cheeks. Why did I have to say 'drugstore'?

"Like after-shave or something."

"Good idea." He picked up the menu and began to study it. "What's your favorite thing at La Familia?"

"The heuvos rancheros."

"Perfect."

We were the only customers in the place so our food arrived more or less instantaneously. I tried not to stare at Zeke as we ate, but I more or less devoured his appearance along with my eggs, beans and rice. Zeke had slightly bushy eye-brows but no mustache, no beard, no extraneous facial hair. He sat before me clean-shaven and I realized he must have shaved in the restroom of the last Trailways stop before Chillicothe.

"I used to have a mustache," he offered, seeming to read my mind. "But a former ladyfriend pointed out mustaches and beards add years to your appearance." Zeke's smile is sheepish. "Obviously, I'm well past those years when a boy wants to look older."

I like that he eats with his fork in his right hand. That seems comfortable to me, even though I have been making attempts at keeping my own fork in my left hand—the way Brandon does. Zeke asks me about the men in my life.

"Brandon is the principal at Chillicothe High. We go out sometimes," is the answer I had rehearsed and now deliver.

I don't ask about the women in Zeke's life. Something in me doesn't want to know.

Brandon has lived right here in Chillicothe his whole life, and so have I. I know his mom; she comes into the library on a weekly basis—always checking out the latest James Patterson mystery. Brandon's sister, Peggy, was in my class at Chillicothe High. Brandon and I know almost everything about each other; he likes to say we're a "matched set." Of what, I'm not sure.

"What does Brandon think of my coming to visit?" asked Zeke, raising one of those thick eyebrows.

"He's not real happy about it." I couldn't *not* tell Brandon what I was up to. Surely, in this town, word would get out and then he'd think I was sneaking around behind his back. Brandon deserves better than that.

Brandon is a good person. Good family, good job, and even kind of good-looking. He's what you might call a leader in the community. In fact, whenever we go anywhere, he leads—virtually. He walks ahead, leading the way. It kind of irks me.

"What's wrong with this Brandon guy?" Zeke asked.

"Nothing."

The other eyebrow went up.

"Am I one last fling before you settle down like a proper young lady?"

I bent my face to my huevos rancheros.

"Because I have to warn you—I didn't come prepared to unleash fifty shades of grey or purple or any other color on Chillicothe."

I forced myself to look up then and Zeke is grinning. I giggled like a relieved schoolgirl.

The waitress brought the check; Zeke paid and I left the tip. Then we headed back to my car so I could take Zeke to my place. I realized whatever qualms I may have had were dispelled by our friendly lunch. Zeke had been smart to make that suggestion.

"This is quite a place," Zeke commented as we turned in the short driveway at 432 River Street, the only address I've ever had except when I was a short distance away at Knox College in Galesburg.

"It's been in the family for generations, my father's family— my mother was from Waukesha."

The big yellow house sits comparatively close to the street so it's more imposing than its tall two-story structure might otherwise be. There are old photos depicting more front lawn, but when the blacktopped street replaced a country lane, something had to go and with the river on the other side, it was our yard that got short-shrift.

"Must require a bunch of upkeep," Zeke observed.

"It does that, but the rent's free—so it kind of evens out," I pointed out, reluctant to get into the struggles of stretching a librarian's salary over heating bills when a severe winter hit.

I spent most of my free time the week before in a cleaning frenzy, so the front hall gleamed when we entered, a long expanse of honey-colored oak. Even though I usually go in the side door, I wanted Zeke to get the full effect, so we went in off the wide sweep of the front porch, through the double doors—or at least, the one that still opens.

Zeke let out a low appreciative whistle. "Even more impressive inside."

"I'll show you your room," I said, and self-consciously led him up the stairs to the front bedroom where there's a view of the river over the trees.

"Thanks very much, ma'am." Zeke doffed his cowboy hat in a kind of exaggerated bow.

"There's a bathroom right across the hall."

"This'll do very nicely. Will we be sharing the bathroom or can I dump my toothbrush and stuff in there? These old houses don't usually have multiple bathrooms."

"Uh, no. I sleep downstairs and there's a bath down there." I've learned it's cooler in mid-Illinois summers to sleep in what was probably once a maid's room at the back of the house; it helps keep air-conditioning use to a minimum. "I'll be downstairs when you're ready to go for that walk."

I left Zeke to settle in and scurried downstairs to change my shoes. The brown Bass sandals I live in from May through September don't make much of a fashion statement, but they're much more comfortable than the new green flats.

When Zeke reappeared downstairs, we decided to leave the car in the drive and just walk the mile or so into downtown. It was a perfect day, sunny and clean after a dreary rainy week.

"This is a pretty town," Zeke offered, as we passed by the still-operating movie theater.

"It is, isn't it? And, thankfully, it's too early in the season for the sandflies that can be pesky along the river over summer."

"I guess no place is perfect, but Durango comes close."

"I've never been to Colorado, but it looks beautiful in pictures." I, of course, Googled Durango after beginning to trade emails with Zeke.

"It is. Colorado is spectacular, and Durango is one of its prettiest towns," he said, managing to make it sound matter-of-fact, not boastful. He walked beside me, and then once again nonchalantly took my elbow when we crossed the street.

I showed Zeke the library where I work, still in the antiquated Carnegie building downtown. "Should we go in and take a look around?" he asked.

"Not today." He would be on display the minute we walked through the front door and I didn't want to put him through that just yet.

"Is there a place to get an ice cream?" he asked, and so we headed around the corner and down the block to Anderson's. Just as we were about to go in, out came Brandon.

Of course. How did I think I was going to get away with showing Zeke around town without running into Brandon? He would be making an effort to be visible, and there are only so many square blocks in this town.

"Hi, there," Brandon said to me while looking Zeke over.

"Zeke, this is my friend Brandon. Brandon, this is Zeke." I didn't think last names were necessary. Brandon looked a little taken aback at being described as 'my friend.' There was an awkward pause.

"Nice to meet you," Zeke stuck out his hand to Brandon.

"Likewise," said Brandon, hesitating just a moment before shaking Zeke's hand, while giving me a look that said "Really?"

Another pause.

"I'm just giving Zeke a walking tour of Chillicothe's down-town," I said, filling in the open space.

"Thought we'd get some ice cream," Zeke offered.

Pause.

"Well, you've come to the right place." Brandon sort of, kind of, stepped aside.

"Thanks." Zeke again put that sturdy hand of his under my elbow and did a neat sidestep to get us by Brandon, then held the door open for me so we could escape into the ice cream shop.

I could feel Brandon still watching us through Anderson's window but Zeke nudged me down the counter so we could view the flavors on display. He stopped when we got pretty much out of sight of the window. "You okay?"

"Sure. Sorry, I should have known that would happen."

"If you're okay, I'm okay. No skin off my nose." Zeke turned toward the case; "Hey, look, they've got an hon-est-to-god strawberry. I love strawberry." He grinned happily. "What are you gonna have?"

I had done some careful planning about where to go with Zeke. I knew there was a track meet in Canton beginning at four-thirty that afternoon so Brandon would be out-of-town—he went to all the athletic events he could possibly attend. I figured Zeke and I would stay in town and do the fish fry at the River Inn for Friday night's supper, and save our fancier dinner for Saturday night when we could drive down along the river to Peoria. With Brandon at the track meet, he wouldn't just happen to walk in on us at the River Inn, which was a short drive from my house on the north side of Chillicothe.

But it's a small town. "Hi, Karen," said Marlene, who enjoyed her role as River Inn hostess. She and her husband

Ward owned the place. "Just the two of you?" She eyed Zeke with obvious curiosity.

"Could we have that booth furthest from the bar?" I asked, pointing.

"Sure thing." Her look said *I get it. You're not fooling me, honey.*

Zeke and I followed her sashaying hips to the most remote corner of the place, where she deposited us along with a pair of laminated menus. "The Deep-Fried Cod is our Friday Night Special for just 9.99. All you can eat, includes fries and coleslaw," she told Zeke. "Enjoy." She smiled at him and winked at me.

"Are you ashamed to be seen with a cowboy?" Zeke asked, seemingly amused by my attempt to park us at a table where we would escape notice.

"No. It's not that." I searched for an explanation. "I just don't want you to have everyone staring at you."

"It's okay, I'm used to the spotlight."

"You are?"

"Sure. I told you, I'm a cowboy poet. I get up and spout nonsense in front of bunches of people—sometimes in a bar, sometimes in a book store, sometimes even in a library."

"I could never do that."

"That's fine, as long as you sit in the audience and applaud."

It was easy to imagine Zeke entertaining a crowd. "I hope I get to see you perform sometime."

"Me too." Zeke grinned at me, then picked up the menu. "Do we even need these things, or are we having the fish fry?"

"It's pretty good," I admitted.

"You a beer drinker? Should we order a pitcher of beer?"

"Why not?" My sense of adventure seemed to call for some sort of alcoholic reinforcement. What do they call it?

False courage, maybe. I didn't know what I expected to happen before the night was over, or even what I wanted to happen. Stumbling across the *heartsafire.com* website had made me curious. And even though I've lived in this town all my life, and had the security of Brandon as an escort just about whenever I wanted, I had come to realize I wasn't happy with our relationship. I wanted something more.

Our waitress turned out to be Shelley, another Chillicothe native, who deposited a couple of glasses of water while studying Zeke, the stranger in town. "You two ready to order?" she asked, leaning over the table to display her considerable attributes to best advantage.

"We'll have two orders of your famous fish fry, and a pitcher of your finest ale," proclaimed Zeke, carefully keeping his eyes on Shelley's eyes.

"Okee-doke," She didn't need to write that down—just stuck her pencil behind her ear and sauntered off.

Our beer arrived almost immediately, followed by the cod served on sturdy thick oval-shaped white diner plates.

"I think they have these same kind of plates at the place I go for fish-fry in Durango," Zeke marveled. "Must be a requirement. Plain food, plain plates. No pretense. I like that."

There was so much I wanted to know about Zeke. And the more I was with him, the more I wanted to know.

"How come you took the Trailways bus here? Don't you have a car?" I asked as I vigorously salted my fries.

"Yeah, I have an old Jeep. But it's not totally reliable so I didn't want to take her on a long road trip. I suppose I should trade her in, but I'm kind of attached to her." He took the salt shaker from me and went after his fish and fries, even giving his glass of beer a sprinkle. "Besides, I like to ride the bus."

"You do?"

"Yup. I can look at the scenery instead of worrying about driving. And I love the other passengers—they're invariably interesting, great fodder for any kind of writer."

I decided not to ask Zeke if he was a repeat customer with *heartsafire*. This had all the makings of a new beginning for me, and I hoped it did for him.

I like beer—especially with fried fish—but I was careful not to drink too much; I wanted (a) to be able to responsibly drive us back to my place, and (b) be fully aware of all that was happening. I knew as the night progressed, I wouldn't want to forget a moment. We lingered over supper, neither of us in a rush.

But when we got home, as soon as we were inside the door, Zeke pulled me to him and gave me a lingering kiss. I succumbed, happily. "I hope you don't mind," he said. "I've been wanting to do that all night."

I answered by kissing him back. He was stronger than he looked, solid. With his arms around me, I somehow felt totally embraced. Cared for.

"Let me show you where I bunk," I said, and led him back through the kitchen to my room.

This wasn't a routine tumble in the hay, which is what I kind of felt sex with Brandon was. This was an occasion to remember—the difference between just plain sex and truly making love. Zeke began with tender kisses on my eyelids, then caressed my shoulders, kissed my breasts, as if opening a gift. He was unhurried, seemingly intent upon relishing every moment. The sweetness of the exploration made the culmination all the more exhilarating. I don't have a lot of experience, but I'm not a total babe in the woods either, and that was definitely the best love-making I've ever experienced. At the ripe old age of forty-one. Imagine.

I know there was a smile on my face the next morning. I reached over to Zeke and opened my eyes at the same time. But he wasn't there. Probably went upstairs when I started to snore. I slipped into my nightgown and quietly went to find him, padding upstairs in my bare feet.

The door to his room was open, and Zeke was... gone. The bed was made—did he even sleep in it? Was the sex that bad? Maybe he just went to get us coffee. But there was no sign of his bag. Then I saw it—propped up on the dresser. A note. Uh-oh, this was not good.

It wasn't just a note, it was a poem:

Dear Karen, sweet librarian
Who could have guessed such a joyful night
Would present me with this fearful plight?
What should have been just play
Hooked me more than I can say!
So I face a predicament
Be a part of your experiment?
Stay, enjoy the rest of our weekend
Wondering if we would see each other again?
I'm so sorry, but I must depart
I'm too old to risk a broken heart.

My heart dropped. I sat on the bed with Zeke's poem clutched in my trembling hand. Now what?

I could fall back on the bed in a melodramatic fit of sobbing. Or I could *not* do that.

I rushed downstairs, took a quick shower, threw some things in a small suitcase, and was at the Trailways bus station within a half-hour, forty-five minutes, tops.

"When is your next bus to Durango, Colorado?" I asked Bernie, the single employee stationed in Chillicothe.

"Popular place," he commented.

"Where do you think you're going?" a voice behind me asked.

I turned, and there stood Zeke. "The next bus isn't 'til 10:30," Zeke said, a little sheepishly.

"Oh, good. I'm in time." I put a hand on his arm as if to detain him.

"What are you up to?" he asked.

"I think I'm running away from home." I kissed him then, right in front of Bernie and everybody. Well, in front of Bernie—there wasn't anybody else at the station.

"Are you sure about this?" Zeke looked skeptical.

"No, I'm not sure. How can anybody be certain about something that's happening so fast? But I *am* certain I will regret not taking a chance on us. Shouldn't we? Won't you at least let me see what Durango looks like?"

I could see Zeke turning matters over in that heart of his. Mine beat rapidly, awaiting his decision.

"If you're too old for a broken heart, I'm too old to pass up what could be the best thing that's ever happened to me," I implored.

An eternity elapsed. Then…

"We should take your car, y'know." Zeke kissed me back. "Then if we felt like stopping to neck, we could do that. Whenever we want."

"Sounds good to me."

Zeke picked up my suitcase and his bag.

"Bye, Bernie," I said. He looked like it was the most normal thing in the world when I followed Zeke out the door to the parking lot.

"Why don't you drive?" I suggested. We got in the car and kissed some more. Then Zeke turned the key in the ignition and pulled out of the parking lot.

As I sat back in my seat and we drove out of Chillicothe, it didn't feel like I was running *away* from some place, as much as it did I was traveling *to* a new place.

Brandon

So one day she's here and the next she vanishes into thin air. One day she's a sensible librarian showing up for work every day and then she's run off to Durango with some cowboy.

Bernie at the bus station told me she was all set to buy a bus ticket but instead the two of 'em just drove off together in her car.

And I have to admit, I don't understand it at all. I thought Karen and I were a couple. Heck, I was even thinking about popping the question, seeing as how we'd been going out for four or five years now. Not exactly sure how long, but it was soon after I got the job at the high school. We've known each other forever, since we were little kids, both growing up in the same town and all. Then we started dating and I just kind of assumed we would end up getting married. Although we're both probably too old to start raising a family.

Karen said something to that effect a while back—that her biological clock was ticking away or something. Didn't bother me none; I've got enough on my hands dealing with a bunch of hormone-happy teenagers over at the school; don't need to add any more to the world's population.

So now what am I supposed to do? It's not like there's an overabundance of eligible females in this town. Karen might not have been the most attractive woman, but she was easy-going, practical, and she had her own place—which made it handy when we were feeling romantic. Couldn't really go back to my house, what with Mom being there and all.

At least I thought she was practical. What kind of business is that—running off with a cowboy? Came to Chillicothe on a Trailways bus, for chrissakes. Probably doesn't even have a real job, much less a car.

Now see, that's just another example of why it's so hard to figure out women. It's been a week and I thought sure she'd have come to her senses and be back by now. I would have forgiven her, probably. I mean, I'd let her explain herself. I'm a reasonable human being. With a real job.

But here I am at the library, checking to see if she's shown up for work. I drove by her house but there's no car in the drive so I thought I'd stop here just in case.

"May I help you find something, Brandon?" It was Eileen Whitcliff, the other librarian and Karen's buddy.

"Um, no. Not really."

"Karen's not here."

"Doesn't look like it." I hated to ask, because it seems like I should have been the one to know, but… "Have you heard from her?"

"She did call and say she needed to take a few weeks off."

"Really…"

"Didn't give any specific date she'd be back."

"But it sounded like she planned on coming back?" I hated the way my voice sounded asking that. Squeaky.

"Not sure about that." Eileen gave me a look I'm guessing she meant to be sympathetic.

Not sure I appreciate being the recipient of sympathy. Maybe Eileen knew more than she was letting on.

"My cell's been on the fritz off-and-on," I told her. "So if Karen's been trying to reach me, I may have missed her call."

If anything, Eileen's look became even more sympathetic. She definitely was withholding information.

"I'm a big boy, I can take it."

"I don't think she's coming back anytime soon, Brandon. She told me to look for some additional help to give me some back-up here at the library."

I sucked in a breath, turned away so whatever look was on my face was one Eileen wouldn't report back to Karen.

"Kind of took us all by surprise," Eileen said.

"Sure as hell did!" I blurted out. I got hold of myself after a second or two. "Sorry. It's not your fault, you're just the messenger."

"I don't like to be the bearer of bad news. Especially to one of my favorite people."

Huh? I'm one of Eileen Whitlock's 'favorite people?'

"Frankly, I don't understand what Karen's up to at all," Eileen confided. "Seemed to me she had a pretty good situation here."

That's what I thought.

"Some people always think the grass is greener on the other side, I guess," Eileen observed.

So it really wasn't my fault.

"Probably wasn't anything anybody here did," she said. "Maybe Karen is having one of those midlife crises?"

"Isn't she a little young for that?"

"Well, I know she's a few years older than me." Eileen smiled so I'd know she was just being helpful.

"How long do you think one of those things lasts?" I asked.

"Oh, gosh knows! She could be back next week…or she could never come back."

"Really? You think she'd give up her nice house and a good job just because she had some sort of crisis thing?"

"People have done stranger things."

"I guess." I thought then about my cousin Phil who moved off to somewhere out east thinking he was actually going to make a living as a poet. Phil was a little strange in more ways than one.

I studied Eileen, who was pleasant-enough looking, and—as she said—a little younger than Karen. "Would you ever do anything like that?"

"Me? Oh, gosh no. I like it here. I mean, I don't have a boyfriend or anything, which would make my life even better, but I'm happy living in this nice little town where everybody knows everybody else."

"Me, too. It's friendly, isn't it?"

"It is, yes."

I tried to remember what I knew about Eileen. "How long have you worked here at the library?"

"Ever since I finished school at SIU. It's the only job I've ever had."

"And you like it?"

"I do. It's changing some, what with the Internet and everything, but that just makes my work more challenging. More exciting."

"Right." Eileen seems like a woman who's got her head on straight.

"What time do you get off work?" I asked.

Welcome to the Real World

Grace had been up for what seemed like hours when she finally heard Jerrod in the bathroom. Eventually he shuffled into the kitchen, wearing only the tattoo of an eagle on his left shoulder.

"Is there coffee?" he asked.

"Put some clothes on," she said, glancing quickly away from him. She studied the view out the window over the kitchen sink—the familiar wide expanse of lawn that led down to the lake's edge, just turning green again after a long Wisconsin winter.

"You liked me naked just fine last night," he said. Jerrod moved up close behind her, interrupting the pretty reverie she'd been having…images from her childhood, swinging in the tire that still hung by a rope from the huge fir tree in the backyard of her grandmother's cottage.

"Naked between the sheets is one thing," Grace said, keeping her back to him. "Walking around my kitchen in broad daylight is another."

"Maybe you're not the wild woman I thought you were," Jerrod said, pressing against her backside.

She turned to face him then, slid her hands around to grab his firm butt, pulled him close and grinned. "I thought you were after a cup of coffee?"

"Coffee can wait." Jerrod picked her up and carried her into the bedroom and dropped her into the tangled sheets that still held the scent of last night's sex.

Afterward, as the two of them lay between soft yellow sheets, Grace looked about—smug, content. April's thin sunlight slid through the fragile lace curtains at the windows. Jerrod dozed. Grace watched his lazy breathing; this was only the second time they'd spent an entire night together. She wondered what her grandmother would have thought—after all, they were lying in her grandmother's bed. Grace's grandmother had died four years ago, outliving Grandpa Carl by just a few years. The family had sold her grandparents' place in town, but kept the treasured lake cottage.

Lucky for Grace. She had moved into the cottage full-time in January, when she found a job at the hardware store in town. Her bachelor's degree in Anthropology didn't help much in the current job market—people were still being laid off, not hired. Grace knew many of her classmates were similarly making do, even her bright and talented roommates—Sasha was a barista in one of Madison's many coffee houses, Caroline had taken a job as a nanny for a family on Lake Shore Drive in Chicago.

Grace felt fortunate to have found the minimum-wage job that meant she could pay for her own groceries, gasoline and miscellaneous expenses while she lived rent-free in her grandparents' cottage. Family members made it clear she wouldn't have the place to herself over the summer, but this was April in northern Wisconsin, they were still likely to get snow. Best of all, she was no longer under her parents' roof. During the six months after she finished school in Madison, she had no place to go but home to Oshkosh—an experience she found both frustrating and mortifying.

"They still want to know where I'm going, who I'm going with," Grace had complained to Caroline. "I'm a college graduate…an adult…and they treat me as if I'm still in high school."

"You'll always be their little girl," Caroline teased.

So Grace relished the independence she enjoyed now in this comfortable cottage. While it wasn't quite the career-woman-condo she had envisioned—an apartment near an ivy-covered campus, perhaps—it was, at least temporarily, a place of her own.

The cottage gave her privacy, but the small town didn't give her much of a social life. Jerrod represented the total sum of anything resembling dating that was happening for her. She was first attracted to him because he was so drop-dead physically gorgeous—dark-haired and lean-bodied. Grace was delighted when it became obvious he was flirting with her during his visits to the hardware store.

Sasha, who had two older brothers and was thus an expert on men, listened to Grace prattle on about Jerrod and his breathtaking good looks.

"He's trouble," Sasha intoned.

"You sound like my mother," Grace complained.

"Just be careful," Sasha said. "He's probably had his way with women since he's been in grade school. Don't expect this guy to stick around and parent your babies."

Now Grace studied the sleeping Jerrod a minute longer. It was clear his good looks gave him a healthy dose of self-confidence, an ability to seize the moment—to make love in the middle of the day, for instance. She liked that about Jerrod. Grace was in no rush to walk down the aisle, but she'd really like to have a boyfriend. Someone to spend some time with, see movies, do some hiking, and maybe—eventually—introduce to the family. She'd had a couple romantic relationships in college but they didn't last very long and hadn't turned out to be all that meaningful; she felt ready for something a little more "adult."

Grace slid quietly out of bed, gathered up her clothes and headed for the bathroom to take a quick shower. She hadn't taken one earlier because she didn't wanted to wake Jerrod. Now, even though it was Tuesday, her day off, she thought it was way past time for both of them to be up—it being almost noon.

Jerrod was a regular at Freitag's Hardware even before Grace started working there. The store was an old family business, surviving in spite of the chains; Grace liked that you could still buy just four nails if that was all you needed. Freitag's carried almost as much in the way of sporting goods—mostly hunting and fishing equipment—as it did in actual hardware. Jerrod, who supported himself by doing what he called construction work, primarily home repairs, was a purchaser of both hardware and sporting goods—a new lockset for somebody's door, or shells for his sixteen-gauge shotgun. He rented a room over the Paradise Bar & Grill in the next block, so Freitag's was very handy. Still, his visits to the store became noticeably more frequent as January eased into February. He made his move in early March.

"I don't really have any jobs this week; maybe I should paint my own place," he said on a cold grey Monday. "What do you think?"

"Do you like to paint?" Grace asked.

"Not really, but maybe it'd keep me out of trouble." He grinned at her in a conspiratorial manner she found most attractive. "What color do you think I should paint it?"

"Maybe you should take some color chips home and see what looks best in whatever light you have," she suggested. She sounded as if she knew what she was talking about.

"Good idea!" he said, and managed to make three or four stops in the store in just that one week, bringing back a couple of strips that "didn't look so good," and picking up new ones.

"Do you think you could you come over after work and take a look—be my color consultant?" Jerrod suggested toward the end of that week. "Most women have a better sense of color than men anyway, don't they?" He even offered to spring for hamburgers at the Paradise Bar & Grill.

Grace pretended to contemplate the idea.

He stopped by when she got off work to walk Grace over to his place. And she figured it was according to plan when, after going through the motions of holding color chips to the walls, after burgers and a few beers down at the Paradise, he suggested they go back upstairs to his apartment to check out how the color they'd chosen would look under artificial light.

"After all, most of the time I spend there is at night, when I'm not working," Jerrod pointed out.

Naturally, she'd acquiesced. How could she not, when he proved to be such an imaginative schemer? And, as she had suspected, the sex proved to be very good, too. He never did get around to painting his place.

Apparently, there were no urgent home repairs to be made on this fine day, because Jerrod continued to snooze even though Grace made no attempt to be quiet—leaving the bedroom door open as she went back into the kitchen and started making breakfast, or lunch, or whatever it was. Since Jerrod had stayed over on Monday night the previous week—what with Tuesday being her day off—she'd antici-pated this might possibly happen again this week, and had picked up both bacon and eggs when she stopped at the grocery store.

The smell of bacon frying in the skillet did the trick. She heard the shower running just as she turned the strips over the first time.

On impulse, Grace went into the living/dining room and took a couple of dinner plates out of a built-in corner cabinet. When Grace's grandparents began to spend months at a time at their beloved cottage, they winterized the place, and moved more and more of their things out here. Things like her grandmother's good china, which they used whenever friends or family came for dinner.

Grace had always liked her grandmother's good china: not terribly ornate, it had a narrow gold rim encircling a border of tiny blue-green flowers. And she liked the idea of using these dishes now—on an ordinary Tuesday—rather than saving them for "company dinner."

Grace set the plates on the unused back burner of the stove to warm them up a little and poured herself a cup of coffee. She wrapped both hands around the smoothness of her pretty blue ceramic mug, inhaled the fabulous scent of the hazelnut-flavored blend Sasha had given her, and breathed a contented sigh.

"Hey, I could get used to this," the now-clothed Jerrod said, picking up a piece of bacon from the batch draining on paper towels.

"Get yourself a coffee mug from the cupboard to your right," Grace said. "How do you like your eggs?"

"You did the bacon, I'll do the eggs," Jerrod said, surprising Grace. She hadn't pictured him doing any cooking—and she *had* pictured the lovely Jerrod doing any number of things more than a few times over the past couple of weeks.

"Okay, I'll make some toast," she said, willingly relinquishing the spatula to Jerrod. "I like mine over-easy…and I'll have two, please."

"Oh, naturally. 'Over easy.' Couldn't be anything simple like scrambled."

"I'll do it, if you want. You can make the toast." Grace reached to take back the spatula.

"No...no I can handle it," Jerrod said, pulling the spatula back behind him. "Matter of fact, 'over easy' is one of my specialties."

Grace wondered if he meant for that to sound so sexy. Then she saw the way he was grinning at her and she actually felt a warm blush rising in her cheeks then turned quickly away to busy herself making toast.

As it turned out, Jerrod was good at making eggs over-easy because that's the way he liked his own. "Am I supposed to use these fancy plates here?" he asked, as he delicately flipped each of the four eggs and was ready to remove them from the skillet.

"Right," Grace said. "Those were my grandmother's plates."

"Pretty fancy for bacon and eggs."

"It'll make them taste even better—you'll see." Grace poured a little more coffee in each of their mugs and sat down at the round wood kitchen table.

"I thought maybe we were going to have to eat in the dining room," Jerrod said, smirking and setting plates at each of their places, then easing into the chair across from Grace.

"You can eat in the dining room if you want," she said.

"Now, now. Be a good girl and eat your breakfast." Jerrod wagged his fork at her, then eagerly stabbed the yolk of his first egg and dipped a piece of toast into it.

Grace happily worked her way around the yolks of both her eggs, eating the whites in small separate bites.

"What are you doing?" Jerrod asked. "I guarantee those yolks are okay to eat. Look, mine's perfect."

"Oh, I'm sure they're fine. This is the way I always eat my eggs. My grandfather taught me; it's the best way to eat fried eggs. You save the yolks for last and then eat them with the toast."

Jerrod looked at her and shook his head.

"Don't knock it 'til you've tried it," Grace said. Now that the preliminaries—the whites—were out of the way, she poked first one yolk and then the other with her whole wheat toast, spooning the runny yolk onto the toast and popping it into her mouth. "Mmmmm," she said, elaborately licking her lips and grinning at Jerrod.

"Weird," he proclaimed. "It's like a little kid who doesn't want his peas to touch his mashed potatoes." He rose from the table and set his plate in the sink, then came back to watch her clean the last bit of yolk off her plate with a crust of toast. "What'll we do today?"

"You don't have to work?" she asked.

"I'm all yours, baby."

"Well, in that case…" Grace rose and put her plate in the sink. "First we can do the dishes…" she paused. "And then we can play a game of croquet."

"Croquet!?" Jerrod looked at her in disbelief. "Croquet is for sissies or little kids. Don't you have a football? We could toss that around."

"Oh, you're just afraid I'll whip your butt," Grace said. "Tell you what, I'll do the dishes and you go out to the garage for the croquet set. You could have it all set up by the time I'm finished here."

"Maybe I can find a football, or at least a ball and bat," Jerrod said, and headed out the back door. "I'm not playing any girlie games."

Grace peered out the window as she filled the sink with hot water and dish soap. She felt almost as if she was 'playing house' as she watched Jerrod amble over to the small barn that doubled as a garage. Jerrod pulled open the door and disappeared inside. Last night, he had parked his F-150 in there after he followed her home from town; it had looked as if it might rain and he had a bunch of stuff in the bed of the truck that he didn't want to get wet. At least that's what he said; Grace wondered then if there was some other woman he didn't want to have find out he was spending the night.

She poured the last of the coffee into her mug, then took the grounds out to throw them over the bed of irises just outside the back door. It would be a while before the irises bloomed—just now they were bright green shoots poking up out of the dark dirt—Post-It notes for spring. She knew irises thrived on coffee grounds; her grandmother and her own mother had been depositing them there for decades.

As she went back in the house and returned to the sink, she saw Jerrod going out of the barn. He appeared to be carrying a box of some sort, but his back was to her and she couldn't figure out what it was. Maybe he had found the croquet set and was going to humor her after all. With just a few steps, he was out of sight around the corner of the barn.

The summer Grace turned twelve, she discovered what a good croquet player her grandmother was. Croquet was the game of choice whenever the extended family gathered at the lake cottage—often to celebrate Grace's July 3 birthday in combination with the Fourth; fireworks were clearly visible across the lake. Grace grew to recognize that she received special attention as the youngest grandchild, but she honestly didn't realize there had been a loving conspiracy—led by her grandmother—that allowed Grace to frequently win the croquet games. It was cleverly done, with close games and near misses, and sometimes arranging for her to come in second so she would demand a rematch. Then, the day after her twelfth birthday, her grandmother turned into an Olympic champion of the game, demolishing the competition. And Grace realized she'd been snookered all those years.

"You're a big girl now, Grace," her grandmother had explained, raising her mallet in victory after a lopsided win. "Welcome to the real world!" She gave Grace a generous hug.

Grandpa had chimed in. "I'm sure it'll only be a few years before you'll be winning for real, Gracie. Someone's gotta take her down a peg."

And he was right. Grace practiced every chance she got while she visited the lake cottage over the next few summers, and when she was sixteen, she was declared the legitimate winner of the family croquet tournament. Afterward, they all gathered for her birthday dinner—served on the good china, of course—with Grace's favorite strawberry shortcake for dessert. Her grandmother stuck a candle in everyone's portion, and they each blew out their own after they'd sung "Happy Birthday."

Grace finished washing up the breakfast things and left them to drain in the dish rack, except for the two good plates, which she carefully dried and returned to their places in the china cabinet. She went into the bathroom to run a brush through her hair and heard a loud BLAM! It sounded like a gunshot.

Grace ran out the back door, terrified of what she might find. She wondered where her cell phone was. Another BLAM! came from back of the barn. She ran over to the barn, stopped, and then cautiously edged her way down the side of it. Was someone trying to steal Jerrod's truck?

But no. As she peeked around the corner of the barn, there was Jerrod, firing his sixteen-gauge at targets that he had set up along a piece of rail fence on the far side of the yard.

"What are you doing?!" Grace shrieked. She couldn't remember ever hearing a gun fired out here in this tranquil haven.

Jerrod turned around, a satisfied grin on his face. "Just getting in a little target practice, babe. In case I need to bag us a turkey or protect you from the raccoons."

Grace stormed over to him and attempted to grab the shotgun away from him. "You can't do that here. This isn't a shooting range!"

Jerrod hung onto his weapon. "Hey! I'm not hurting anybody. There's nobody else around. This is a perfect place for practicing—and those old plates I found make just the right size target from this distance."

Now Grace looked over at the fence. There were nine plates lined up on the rail second from the top. On the new spring grass, there were a few remnants of one plate that had been blown to smithereens. Jerrod had obviously missed with his first attempt, but scored a bullseye on the second. A large cardboard box sat in the grass at the end of the line of plates, surrounded by mounds of rumpled tissue paper—a safe house having been plundered.

"See, they're just the right size to sit on that second rail, and the tops of them reach to lean against the top rail," Jerrod proudly pointed out.

Grace walked over to the fence and looked at the plates. She thought she would be sick right there in the dazzling green grass. She turned toward Jerrod, barely able to speak. "These… these are…my grandmother's good plates."

"Hey, the box says 'extra plates,'" Jerrod said. "They're extras. They can't be all that special if they're in the garage instead of in that cupboard in the house."

"Because there isn't enough room, you idiot!" Grace picked up one of the plates and waved it at Jerrod. "These are the plates we need when the whole family gets together."

"It says 'extra' on the box," Jerrod said, pointing to the box as if it were the box's fault.

Grace strode over to the box and started stuffing some of the tissue back into it, all the while hanging onto the plate she had waved at Jerrod. She could feel tears ready to burst forth, but she really, really didn't want to cry. "You could have asked. Any person with half a brain would have asked."

"But then you'd have wanted to play stupid croquet…instead of letting me get in some target practice." Jerrod conjured up what he obviously thought was his most disarming smile and took a few steps toward her.

She turned her back to him and started wrapping the plate in some of the loose tissue. She was trembling with anger—at Jerrod for his stupidity and at herself for crying. Because now she *was* crying, tears streaming down her cheeks.

"Fuck," Jerrod said. "Is there anything in there that I *can* use for target practice?"

Grace whirled around. "You'd better get out of here before I decide you'd make a good target."

"Aw, come on. I didn't mean to make you cry." Jerrod took another couple steps toward her. Tall, lean, dark-haired, good-sex Jerrod. "I can buy you a new plate or two," Jerrod offered, still advancing toward her, still dragging the shotgun along.

"I'm serious, Jerrod. Please. Leave. Now."

He stopped. "But we were having such a great time." Clueless Jerrod.

"We were." Grace realized there was no explaining to him the seriousness of the crime he had committed. He just wouldn't understand. "But our 'great time' has ended."

"You don't mean that." He took another step toward her.

Grace held her hands up in front of her. "I do mean it. Don't take another step this way. Just turn around, get in your truck, and leave." For a minute Grace wondered if she was in serious trouble—just how much had she misjudged the shotgun-toting Jerrod?

"Okay," he said. "I get the message. I still don't understand what the big deal is. But I'm not the kind of guy who hangs around when he's not wanted." He turned and started to walk away, then stopped and looked back at her. "There are other women who do want me around, you know."

"I'm sure they do, Jerrod. I'm just not one of them anymore." She turned back to the fence, grabbed a stray piece of tissue and pulled the box over to where the next plate was propped on the rail. She carefully wrapped it in tissue, put it in the box, and moved to the next plate. Grace heard him start up his truck and back it out of the barn, then shift out of reverse and heard the gravel kick up as he stepped on the gas and roared down the drive to the road. She did not turn around to watch him leave.

Tea and Biscuits

Aunt Miriam didn't believe in air-conditioning, a real pain on unbelievably hot and muggy days in August. I went searching for a cool corner in her big old house. It's the same every summer. I get sent to stay for a week with Aunt Miriam and they call it a "vacation." I finally figured out it's really a vacation for my mother. And some company for Aunt Miriam.

I found a little breeze and some cool shade on the porch swing. If I gently pushed my toe on the floorboards I created even more breeze, so the sweat trickling down the sides of my face sort of went away. Evaporated, I guess. If I sat with my braids lifted up off the back of my neck, it was even better.

Boring. The kids in my fifth grade class at Walker School back in Rockford couldn't believe it. Incredibly boring. Just me and ancient Aunt Miriam rattling around in this ancient house on top of a hill overlooking the dinky town of Galena. She is really my mother's aunt, so that makes her my great-aunt. She has lived all her life in this same house. When Aunt Miriam's parents died, she just stayed here all by herself.

This summer—between fifth and sixth grade—I thought my "vacation" was going to be just as boring as ever, but before it was over things got so interesting I started keeping a journal. Maybe I'll be a famous novelist someday.

"There you are! I wondered where you had gone off to." Aunt Miriam peered through her bifocals from behind the screen door. "Maybe we should have our tea out here?"

Was she really going to go through with her afternoon tea ritual on a day as hot as this?

"It'll be cooler out here." She pushed the door open a little. "Will you help me bring the things out?"

Aunt Miriam is the only person I know who serves Afternoon Tea. "Sweet!" is what my friend Josie called it when I was explaining the things I had to put up with during my week in Galena.

"Sweet? What's sweet about ruining a perfectly good afternoon with a cup of hot tea and stale cookies?"

"It's traditional," Josie pointed out. "Unique. How many people do you know who get to have afternoon tea?"

"Exactly. It may be traditional, but it's also weird."

There was no getting out of it. I had to give up my comfy spot on the porch swing and follow her into the kitchen. The tea was all made, brewed from real tea leaves in the special china teapot now cloaked in a cover you call a "cozy."

"If you'll bring our cups and saucers, Caroline, I'll bring the teapot and our biscuits."

Aunt Miriam calls her rock-hard cookies 'biscuits.' She explained that's what they are called in England, and that's where the cookies are from. No wonder they were so stale, they had to come all the way from across the ocean.

I followed her back out onto the porch, carrying a cup and saucer in each hand. She stood with her back against the screen door and held it open for me to pass through. I sure didn't want to drop one of the special cups or saucers. They were very pretty, with little red roses painted on them, and they made you feel kind of pretty just drinking out of them.

"Now, isn't this nice?" she remarked as she settled in her chair at the little table on the other end of the porch from the swing. "There's a lovely breeze out here, isn't there?"

"Hmm-hmm."

She poured tea into our cups. It smelled of orange and honey, already sweetened with a generous spoonful of honey in the pot, so there was no need to bring a sugar bowl to the table. Did she make her afternoon tea with honey when I wasn't here? Probably not. I reached for a cookie and dunked it in my tea. It was a technique Aunt Miriam had suggested—even though she observed it wasn't truly lady-like.

"These biscuits are good but quite firm; dunking helps soften them," she had first recommended several summers ago. The biscuits were pretty tasty when they were soaked in orange-and-honey tea, but they were small. I took another and dunked it—holding it in my cup a moment to allow it to soak up as much tea as possible before reaching that crucial falling-apart-in-the-cup stage.

A bee buzzed by, hovering over the cookie plate. "He wants his honey back!" exclaimed Aunt Miriam. She waved at him with her napkin. A cloth napkin, of course. She used paper napkins for breakfast and lunch, but cloth napkins for afternoon tea and supper. It was my job to iron the napkins during my week of so-called vacation. Aunt Miriam showed me how last summer. At home, Mom just shakes things out of the dryer and folds them all neat right away or hangs them on hangers so they don't need ironing. But my great-aunt explained that the cloth napkins were not "wash and wear"—that they needed to be sprinkled with water and ironed so they would be perfectly smooth and crisp when you took one from beside your plate and put it in your lap.

The bee floated off to the petunias and Aunt Miriam took a sip of tea. "It's quite good, don't you think?" She took another sip, just to make sure. "I got it from that tea shop on Main Street."

I knew the one she meant, definitely an Aunt-Miriam-kind-of-store. Lots of different kinds of teas, and herbs, and pretty wreaths made out of dried flowers. Aunt Miriam is actually kind of pretty, but you might not notice right away. If you look carefully you see her face is perfectly oval, framed in short brown hair, and she has light brown eyes that seem to almost always be pleased about something. She doesn't look really old although there is some gray in her hair and I know she has to be at least seventy. But she's small and slim, so she looks kind of cute in her NPR t-shirt and capris. Aunt Miriam calls them "pedal pushers."

"How come you don't have a husband?" The words were out of my mouth before I knew it. I did that a lot; Mom was always telling me to think before I speak. So I was always having to apologize. "Oh! I'm sorry. I didn't mean that."

She smiled. "That's all right, dear. It's completely understandable that you might wonder about that. I'm certain many people do." She dunked a biscuit. "And probably some of them have made up some interesting answers for themselves." She munched on her cookie and then offered the plate to me. "A biscuit, dear?"

Well, as long as she offered, might as well have another.

"We might even have our dinner out here," she proposed. "Would you like that?" She stood and began to clear the tea things.

"That'd be nice," I said. I picked up the cups and saucers and followed her back into the kitchen.

Later, as I sat on the porch swing again, I realized Aunt Miriam had never answered that question. Was that when the bee came along? No, I'm pretty sure she had just plain changed the subject. She'd offered me another one of her stale biscuits instead of any kind of explanation.

I thought about that as I sat on the swing holding my braids in the air. The braids had been Aunt Miriam's idea. "I know it's all the fashion to have lots of long hair," she'd said. "But aren't you warm?" Duh. My solution would be to install air-conditioning like we have back home. Instead, my great-aunt showed me how to braid my hair so it didn't *hang down all around my face and neck.* Her words, not mine. "Not only that, it's a very charming look for you," she decided. "See?" And she had handed me the small hand mirror from the kitchen junk drawer.

I've never been called "charming" before. I'm not into being all girly with nail polish and stuff. When I look in the mirror, I guess I don't see *charming*—just dull brown hair and more of the freckles that show up every spring.

"I had freckles just like yours when I was a young girl," Aunt Miriam told me. "I think they're a display of an interesting personality."

Never heard that one before.

The next day is when stuff started happening. I was sitting on the porch steps after lunch when a little rabbit hopped by. He seemed to disappear under the porch. I went down the steps to check it out. Criss-crossed pieces of wood covered the open spaces on either side of the steps with holes big enough for a rabbit to squeeze through. But not big enough for a person. I got on my knees in the flowerbed alongside the steps and peeked through into the dark space under the porch but I couldn't see anything very well. When I poked a finger through I discovered the fencing was kind of shaky. I gave it a little tug. The fence wiggled. I pulled a little harder and a section of the fencing came away at the top. I stood up to get a better look underneath. I couldn't see the bunny, but there was stuff under there. An old bicycle, a couple boxes, and what looked like a shovel or something. So I gave the fencing a good yank and a piece about as wide as me came loose.

The bicycle was kinda rusty and I saw right away that the chain was hanging down off its track so I didn't bother trying to pull it out from under the porch. But what about the two boxes stacked one on top of the other? A spider web went from one corner of the top box to the underside of the steps. I picked up the shovel and brushed the web away. It would be good if I could get them out from the darkness under the steps so I could see what was inside. Would they fall apart if I tried to move them? Hmmm. Well, only one way to find out. I tried to lift the top one. Uhnn. It was *heavy*. Heavier than I thought it was going to be. What was in these things? They weren't big enough to hold a body. Unless it was all chopped up in little pieces.

Scaredy-cat. There wasn't any body in these boxes. That was only in movies.

Even though it was kinda dark under there, I figured there was probably enough light to at least see what kind of stuff was in the box if I just opened it right where it was, without dragging it out into the sunlight. Especially since now my eyes were kind of adjusting to the light. Or the lack of light. The dark.

Were there any more spider webs? I kind of waved the shovel around the boxes another couple of times, just in case.

It was now or never. The boxes were right under the steps so there wasn't much room to maneuver. Very old tape sealed the boxes closed. But I just squeezed my finger under an open section of the flap, pushed up, and the tape gave way. I was kinda hunched under the steps and over the boxes in order to open the flaps and see what was inside. Turned out to be newspaper. A couple of sections of old *Galena Gazettes* covered whatever was underneath. I tossed them aside and looked at—balled up newspapers? No, the newspapers were wrapped around stuff. I poked at one ball. It seemed too hard to be a body part. Unless that rigid mortis stuff had set in. *Stop it! These are not body parts!* I picked up one of them and carefully unwrapped whatever it was, ready to drop it and run if my worst fears were realized.

It was a cup—a china teacup like the ones Aunt Miriam used for afternoon tea. I took it out into the sunlight so I could see it better. It was exactly like her teacups.

I went back into the darkness under the porch steps and discovered more cups, and saucers, and even dinner plates with the same pretty red roses painted on them. Why were they here instead of up in the storeroom? Or, better yet, on the shelves in the pantry? Did she know they were here? I could hardly wait to tell her about my discovery.

But what if Aunt Miriam already knew about them? If she did, why didn't she use them? Was there something wrong with the dishes? They looked good to me. What if this was a secret that nobody was supposed to know except her?

I decided to wrap the dishes back in the newspaper and close up the box. I would think about it this time before I said something. Mom would like that. Maybe I was *maturing*.

"Caroline!" I heard Aunt Miriam call my name from some-where above me. "Caroline?" I heard the screen door open and footsteps on the porch. I held my breath in the dark shadows under the steps. "Are you out here?" Now I could hear her coming down the steps.

"Goodness! What ever are you doing under there, Caro-line?" She bent over to look into the darkness at me.

"There was a rabbit…" I began, as I stood holding a plate in one hand and crumpled newspaper in the other.

She straightened up and stood contemplating the scene, waiting for an explanation.

"I found these dishes...." I held out a plate for her inspection, but she did not come any closer. "Did you know they were here?" I asked.

Still she stood, silent.

"They look exactly like the Afternoon Tea cups and saucers," I pointed out, and stepped out from under the porch to hand her the unwrapped dinner plate. "See?"

Aunt Miriam took the plate carefully in both hands, studying its pretty pattern for a moment, then looking up at me, then looking at the box under the porch, then back at me, and finally again to the plate in her hands.

"They're the same, aren't they?" I asked.

"Yes, dear. They're the same."

"But why are they down here? Did you know they were here?"

"Yes, Caroline. I knew they were here. I put them here myself."

"Really? But why?"

"It's a story from a long time ago, dear." She smiled at me and took the piece of newspaper I still had crumpled in one hand and used it to rewrap the plate. "Why don't you brush yourself off a bit and we'll talk about it over our tea." She turned and went up the steps, carefully carrying the plate in one hand and using the other hand to pull herself up on the porch rail.

I could hardly wait for Afternoon Tea.

We sat on the porch again. My great-aunt had arranged some of her biscuits on a paper doily on the rose-patterned dinner plate that matched our teacups.

"Those dishes were a wedding present," she began. Then she stopped, seemed uncertain how to proceed.

"Whose wedding?" I asked, helpfully.

"Mine."

"But I thought you never got married?"

"I didn't." She took a sip of tea. I could tell this was not a time for me to keep yakking. So I waited.

"I got stood up at the altar," she said, sort of exhaling the words in a rush.

"What do you mean?" I asked.

"I mean…that nearly a hundred family members and friends had been invited to a lovely church wedding and sat waiting in their pews, and I stood waiting in the little room they called 'The Bride's Room,' and the groom just never showed up."

"Oh, my gosh."

"Yes, oh my gosh, indeed. It was to have been a traditional June wedding. There was even a quite nice reception planned for afterward—right here on this grand lawn in front of the house." She gestured at the wide expanse of lush green grass and pretty flowers beyond the porch.

"What did you do?"

"Well, at first we all waited. And waited some more. And then the priest came back to say to me that he thought perhaps the groom had gotten cold feet. Perhaps I'd want my father to make an announcement?" She took off her glasses and wiped at them with her cloth napkin. She looked quite directly at me. "I was too stunned to even cry."

I was too stunned to speak.

"So, eventually my father did make some sort of announcement. It couldn't have been easy for him. And we all left the church and went to our homes. Or, at least I did. I don't know if the others went out and got drunk or what they did."

"Did you get drunk?" I was trying to imagine Aunt Miriam all tipsy.

"No, dear. I didn't. I came home and took off my wedding dress and then went down to the kitchen to help Mother pack up some of the foodstuffs that had been delivered by the Logan House. My father was going to take most of it out to the Poor Farm. Some we kept—we ended up having tea sandwiches for our supper that night. But we didn't keep any of the wedding cake. Mother understood I couldn't bear the sight of it, much less eating any of it. I don't think she could either. She had poured her heart and soul into planning my Big Day. Mother wanted it to be every bit as lovely as Jane's had been three years earlier."

I knew Jane was my grandmother's name, and that she was younger than Aunt Miriam, about seven years younger. I calculated that Aunt Miriam would have been an "older bride."

"Did you ever see him again?"

"Who?"

My usually composed great-aunt seemed to be having difficulty keeping her thoughts together. "The man you were going to marry. The groom."

"No, I never did. He left town. Someone said he went to New Mexico or Arizona or one of those places out west."

"Hmmph." I sounded like my grandmother when she disapproved of someone or something.

"He did write me a letter." She straightened in her chair. "At first my mother wasn't going to give it to me, but my father persuaded her that I was a grown woman and entitled to my personal correspondence."

"What did he say?"

"Well, he apologized, of course. Said he realized he had broken my heart, but that he just couldn't go through with it. That he should have broken it off earlier."

71

"That's right. He shouldn't have just not shown up." I dunked a biscuit in my tea, which by then had cooled off so much it wasn't hot or cold.

"It took me a while—years, I think—to realize that he hadn't actually broken my heart."

"Really?"

"No, he didn't. He embarrassed me. And he embarrassed my family. That's why I packed those dishes away. All the rest of the gifts were returned, but the dishes were from my parents and my mother insisted that I keep them. 'You might want to use them someday,' she said. "But I never did. They were a painful reminder of that awful day. I packed them away—all except for these couple of teacups and saucers—and hid them under the porch so my mother wouldn't see them in the storeroom and suggest, again, that I might want to use them."

"I'm glad you kept a couple out for Afternoon Tea. And I'm glad he didn't break your heart."

"I have a pretty strong heart," Aunt Miriam proclaimed.

"Maybe it's a good thing he, how did you say it? Stood you up at the altar?"

"What do you mean?"

"Well, maybe if you did get married and…everything, maybe you would have had problems later on. Like, if you didn't really love each other? And, if you had kids and then had to get divorced?"

She considered this. "You are very wise, Caroline. That's a very keen observation."

I liked being wise. And keen. "I'm probably not ever going to get married," I said—eager to establish an even closer bond with my great-aunt.

"Oh, you don't want to make that kind of decision now," she cautioned. "You never know what lies ahead. What's important is that when you do make that decision, it's for all the right reasons."

"Not just because I want to have pretty dishes to eat off of."

"Exactly." Aunt Miriam smiled at me. "And now, since you are a very wise young woman," she continued, "let me ask what you think about an idea I have?"

"Okay." I was ready for anything.

"What if, tomorrow morning bright and early, we get Mr. Grosshans over from next door and have him help us bring those two boxes of dishes up to the kitchen?"

"Yes!" I nearly jumped out of my chair.

"It'll be a big chore," she warned. "We'll have to unpack them very carefully, then wash and dry them all. And figure out where to put them—we may have to get rid of some other stuff." She gazed through the screen door into the house as if trying to visualize where her pretty rose-embossed plates would reside.

"But then you'll have them to eat on whenever you want," I reasoned.

"Exactly. They're too pretty to be hiding under the porch. In fact, we just might use them for a celebratory dinner to-morrow night." She smiled at me as if this was my very good idea instead of hers.

"Should we invite anyone else?" I asked.

"Not this time, I don't think. But when your parents come out to pick you up on the weekend, perhaps we should use them for dinner then?"

She was asking my opinion. "Definitely," I said.

A Not-So-Fond Farewell

Therese smuggled two pink Daisy razors into the funeral home so she could do the job herself. Even though she and Ben had known Steve Fitzgerald since high school, Steve was appalled and not about to honor her request. So it was up to her to shave off Ben's mustache. Steve told her they'd have the body all ready the day before the funeral, so she stopped by a little after noon and asked for "some time to be alone with her husband."

She had never liked that mustache and Ben knew it. As the years went by, she pointed out it made him look older, but he thought it was a significant contributor to his overall good looks. He was a big good-looking guy, she had to admit. A little beefier as he aged, but that, too, seemed to contribute to his presence—he was a successful attorney and looked the part.

"Oh, Ben. Ben." Therese contemplated her husband's solemn countenance, betrayed by laugh lines a-plenty. He still had a full head of sandy hair and matching eyebrows, although his mustache had begun to turn grey. Beards and mustaches are always the first to go—but Ben had carefully touched it up with that stuff they advertised on TV. Now she was going to get rid of it once and for all.

It wasn't easy. She didn't have access to soap and water or shaving gel, so she had to dry scrape it off—it was a good thing she thought to bring two razors. She also brought a couple of paper towels so the little hairs wouldn't get all over his shirt after Steve's staff did such a fine job of laying him out.

"There. You look good, you handsome devil." Therese wondered how many people would notice the mustache missing as they went through the visitation line. He had stipulated, a few years back when they made their plans, he wanted an open casket, "unless I've been in an accident and my face gets all mutilated or something." Nope. A heart attack at age sixty-four had done him in, as handsome as ever. Well, almost.

Her mission accomplished, Therese headed home to resume greeting the never-ending trail of visitors coming to the door with pasta salads and brownies.

Elizabeth Newton was in the kitchen when Therese came in the back door. She wasn't a close friend—Therese didn't really have any what you would call "close" friends—but Elizabeth was one of those good souls who showed up when you could use some help and quietly went about the business of doing what needed to be done.

"How did it go?" she asked, as she arranged cookies on one of the good dishes from the dining room hutch.

"Fine."

"Fitzgerald's always does such a beautiful job."

"Yes. Yes, they do," agreed Therese. "I see you're using the good dishes."

"Isn't that what you wanted?" Someone had made lemon squares so now Elizabeth alternated them with brownies in circular rows inside the border of strawberries painted on her fine china.

"Right." Might as well. She had no idea when she would use those dishes again. She tried to imagine her life as a widow and couldn't wrap her head around it.

The front doorbell rang.

"Do you want me to get it?" asked Elizabeth.

"No. I'm here; I might as well see who it is." She hung her purse on a hook in the laundry room just off the kitchen as the bell rang a second time. "Thanks for offering, though."

Marilyn Keating, bearing a lime Jello mold, turned out to be the first of many visitors. Therese greeted neighbors and co-workers and friends and members of her bridge club. At some point, she let others answer the door and took a seat in her favorite chair, the rose-colored wingback she had asked Ben to buy her for Mother's Day a few years ago. Elizabeth took care of any food offerings, taking them into the kitchen, cutting them into serving size pieces and putting them out on the dining room table so people could help themselves. Therese feared this made the visitors stay longer—chatting amongst themselves and sharing food and drink. It was like a party. Ben would have liked to be there. He always liked parties.

She felt like she was going to throw up. She closed her eyes and leaned her head back but that seemed to make her dizzy, so she opened them again and struggled to her feet, then up the stairs to the bathroom. As soon as she closed the door she knew she wasn't going to be sick. She sat down on the closed toilet seat. It would always be closed now Ben wasn't here to leave it up. Guess that's one thing about being a widow. She kind of giggled. What was she doing—giggling? She was the newly bereaved widow of Benjamin Maynard, pillar of the community. She stilled herself for a minute, stood at the sink and slapped a little water on her face, then went back downstairs.

Elizabeth was ushering Carol Stein out the door.

"Where did everybody go?" asked Therese.

"You didn't look so good. I told them you probably needed some rest," Elizabeth said. "I'm going to clean up a few things in the kitchen and then I'll be heading out myself."

"Oh, thank you. Thank you," she murmured.

"I'm glad I can be of help. Are you okay?"

"Yes. I guess I am a little tired."

"Of course you are. But you'll be okay by yourself?"

"Yes. My daughter is due in after dinner, so I won't really be alone."

After Elizabeth had gone, Therese sat at the kitchen table with the pretty plate of food Elizabeth had so thoughtfully fixed for her. She looked at it without really seeing what was there, then got up and poured herself a glass of wine.

Maybe she'd turn into one of those widows who sat at home and drank from noon on. She picked up the fork and began to put food in her mouth, trying to digest the events of the last forty-eight hours. She glanced at the clock. Sara was due home in a little over an hour; how much would she tell her daughter?

When the police officer came to her door the other night, he had been careful about describing the circumstances in which Ben had been found. A 9-1-1 call had been placed from the Timbers Motel and when paramedics arrived, they found Ben, alone and dead of an apparent heart attack. The officer wanted her, or preferably some other family member, to identify Ben's body at the morgue. She would have to go—Sara was the only other immediate family and she lived and worked 1800 miles away in Tucson.

The morgue attendant lifted the sheet from his face. Therese flinched. It was Ben alright. She managed a brief nod, the officer put a hand under her elbow and steered her out of the room, sat her down in a conference room and brought her a cup of coffee.

"Can I call somebody? Do you have a minister or a priest who should be notified?"

Therese shook her head. The coroner came in, obviously summoned from her home to deal with this delicate situation. Therese knew her, liked her. Carol Altamore had been the county coroner for a dozen years or more.

"Therese, I'm so sorry."

Therese nodded. And thus began the litany of sympathies that would crawl through her days while questions crawled through her nights. What was Ben doing at the Timbers? Who was he with? Who made the 9-1-1 call? Apparently it had been made from the front desk in response to a call from the room. A woman's voice. A woman who had vanished as soon as she made the call.

Had Ben hired a prostitute for a one-time fling? Or had he been conducting a long-time affair with someone he worked with? Someone Therese knew?

Therese lied to Steve Fitzgerald, to Elizabeth Newton, to Sara. "They found him sitting in his car in the parking lot at the CVS," she said. The CVS was next door to the Timbers Motel. "He must have felt ill and was going to get some aspirin or something."

Carol Altamore would know the truth, but the compassionate coroner did not mention it as she drove Therese home, nor would she mention it in the days to follow, Therese was pretty sure. Ethical confidentiality or something. There had been no crime committed; there was no need for further police involvement. Unless Therese wanted to pursue the matter.

And she didn't. That much she knew.

For someone so smart, Ben had been pretty stupid. Therese was mad at him about that. The first night, she was numb. But in the hours to follow, and through the next night, she realized she wasn't angry about Ben's having an affair or whatever. She was mad at him for dying. She did love him—and the life they had together. Sure, the romance had gone out of their marriage, they hadn't had sex since she had a knee replacement last year—but that was fine with her. They never talked about it; they merely went on with their day-to-day lives and their sex-free nights. So Therese didn't really know how Ben felt about the lack of sex—maybe he didn't care either. And, she decided if he was having sex elsewhere, it was alright with her as long as she didn't know about it.

But it wasn't alright if it was going to take Ben from her, permanently. Stupid bastard. She drained her glass and got up to pour a little more wine just as Sara arrived. She burst through the front door as if she had run all the way from Arizona.

"Oh, Mom! Oh, oh." She hugged Therese tightly and then let loose a torrent of sobs. "How could this happen?" Sara released her hold on Therese and took a step back. "He was healthy, wasn't he? When was the last time he went to the doctor?"

This was a conversation they already had by phone, so Therese pulled Sara back into a hug and let her cry. Maybe this was the first she had cried. It wouldn't be the last time over these next few days; Sara adored her father. She would never know Ben had been so sure their first and, as it turned out, only child, would be a boy he went out and bought a bat and ball before the child was even born. So naturally Sara turned out to be a tomboy who played catch with her dad as a toddler and pitched for the girls' softball team in high school. Over the years, he took her to several Cubs games at Wrigley Field, even though it was a long car trip. Therese stayed home, recognizing those days as set aside for father-daughter bonding. Not that they needed any special days.

Therese knew she would not reveal any further information to Sara about her father's death. She was angry, but not that angry. Somehow she would get through these next few days—the visitation and service tomorrow and Sara's stay into the weekend—without ruining the image Sara had of her father.

She wanted to put his Cub cap in the coffin with him. Therese agreed it would be something Ben would like, so they took it with them to the funeral home the next morning. Steve Fitzgerald greeted them and ushered them into the parlor where Ben's body lay in its open casket. As he led them to the casket, Steve hesitated and looked carefully at the corpse. His gaze shifted to Therese and she met his look briefly, then turned to Sara. Steve realized she had taken matters into her own hands regarding the mustache; would Sara notice?

"He looks so different," she said.

"Yes," Therese agreed. "Where shall we put the cap?"

Sara had the cap in her hand. "Maybe below his hands?" She put the cap there and then quickly moved it. "No, that looks…weird. I think here, at the side."

"That's good," Therese said.

"I'll leave you two for a bit," Steve said. "People will begin to arrive in fifteen minutes or so, there are always some early birds. Do you want coffee?"

They shook their heads 'no' in unison and he left. Mother and daughter stood with finality closing in on them. Sara began to shed quiet tears.

"Let's sit down." Therese led Sara to the chairs in front, where boxes of tissues were strategically placed.

Elizabeth Newton was the first to arrive; she would not be staying for the service because she would be back at the house, getting ready for those people who would stop by after going to the cemetery. Therese had briefly considered having a luncheon at the club afterward, but decided against it, preferring to greet friends and relatives in the comfort of her own home. She would depend on Elizabeth to shoo them away after a suitable length of time.

The people who had come to the house yesterday had been mostly her friends and acquaintances; now, more of Ben's friends and business associates were arriving to pay their respects. Attorneys, courthouse personnel, a couple of judges, and many clients. People from the office, of course. The visitation had ended and she was seated for the service, with the string trio playing "Amazing Grace," when she realized Ben's secretary, Glendia Nolte, hadn't come through the line. She had been his secretary for ten years—surely she would want to say goodbye to her boss. Therese recalled how helpful Ben was to Glendia when she was divorced a few years back; he hadn't handled the case himself because his area of expertise was tax law, but he had recommended a colleague and pretty much guided her through the ordeal.

Therese turned in her chair, leaning to Sara to say "You okay?" and at the same time looking over her shoulder to survey the rows of people in back of her.

And there she was—Glendia Nolte—seated alone in one of the back rows, not with the rest of the office staff. She looked very, very pale, and Therese had the feeling she had been watching her but looked away when she glanced around.

Quiet, mousy Glendia Nolte? Therese faced forward as the chaplain began to read from scriptures. Words blurred and thoughts smeared. She couldn't be sure, of course. Therese wasn't about to confront Glendia, or anyone else. That would mean admitting her husband had died in disturbing circumstances.

Therese had robbed Ben of his mustache, but he had given her questions she would ask for the rest of her life.

Kuzhi

Adele heard the stagecoach from Kurshan before she saw it. It rattled around the bend in the road and appeared alongside the dark pines that towered at the edge of Kuzhi. Despite the day's feeble drizzle, the team of horses kicked up small clouds of dust before they were brought to a rest by the driver, who clambered down to tie them loosely at the post in front of Yoffe's house. Yoffe's boy came out to lead them to the stream that ran back of the house.

She studied the driver and his motions carefully, but he was empty-handed; no one in Kuzhi would receive a package or a letter today. The driver went along with the boy to take a piss out back and make small talk with Yoffe while the horses drank their fill. Adele shifted her baby from one shoulder to the other and continued to stand watch at the window. When the driver reappeared around the corner of the house, she saw him make his way back to the stage where the lone passenger had now climbed out and was stretching his legs. The driver hiked up to grab something from back of his seat. Perhaps there was a letter after all! But no, he was simply getting his canteen to refill at the little stream.

She turned from the window and put baby Oskar back in his basket. He began to whimper and Adele felt the tears well in her own eyes. It would be another week before the stage came through with any mail—another week before she could possibly expect to hear from her husband, bidding her to "Come now! Come to me in America!"

If only. Would her Leaving Day never come? She blinked back her tears as Chava came bustling into the kitchen with a small pan of potatoes.

"So, no letter today, Addie?" Her older sister was direct, as their mother had been.

"*Neyn.*"

"Maybe next time," Chava said briskly. "You want to scrub these potatoes for me?" *Make yourself useful; stop feeling sorry for yourself*—these were the unspoken words.

Adele nodded and picked up the baby's basket to take it to the back stoop where the little overhang would protect them from the drizzle. She took the pan of potatoes from Chava and gave them a slosh of water from the bucket, grabbed a cloth and a small knife and sat on one of two stools that stood sentry by the door.

She studied the boy's face as she worked. Was it her imagination, or did he look more and more like Jonas every day? She shivered in the cold dampness, then paused to tuck the blanket more securely around him. They had not known she was pregnant when Jonas left for America in early March. She was to stay with her family in Kuzhi—her father and sister only, now that her mother had passed—until he could get himself situated in New York and earn enough money and procure the documents needed for Adele to join him. Before he left, they had been living in beautiful Vilna where Jonas was a pharmacist and they both enjoyed the city's bustling activity.

Jonas, however, was not satisfied with Vilna even. He did not trust the Russians; his parents had been slaughtered in a pogrom while they lived in Chernihiv in the Pale. He escaped death only because he was away at school in Vilna at the time.

Vilna, with its streetcars and electricity and telephones. She certainly wished they were both still there. And the baby. Oskar.

Dear sweet Oskar. Growing bigger and heavier every day. She tried to picture herself carrying him and whatever baggage she would be allowed on the long trip to America. *Abi*. If only.

So much had happened since Jonas left in March. They had traveled together by train from Vilna, and then took the stage to her tiny home village of Kuzhi. After a few days, Jonas went on to Tallinn, the Russian port city on the Baltic Sea where he would board the steamer to America. They planned for Adele to follow him within the year, two years at most. They knew they were working against time; Germany and Russia were waiting for a spark to take them to war. That spark occurred just a few months after Jonas left, on June 28, 1914, when that crazy Serb assassinated the Archduke Ferdinand of Austria. A month later, Austria declared war on Serbia.

Within a week, *a mere week!*—Germany declared war on Russia and France, and then—after Germany invaded Belgium, Britain declared war on Germany. Just to make sure everything was official, Austria declared war on Russia and Serbia declared war on Germany.

Even out here in the middle of nowhere, the news traveled quickly to their tiny village. But Kuzhi was not truly in the middle of nowhere; Kuzhi was in Lithuania, in the middle between Germany and Russia. The farmers ducked their heads and went on working their fields. The six Jewish families of the village huddled together on the Sabbath, praying that whoever eventually won this war would regard their people favorably.

As the harvest was coming to a close—Papa with his scythe in the wheat and Chava carefully bundling her flax for drying—that's when Oskar was born. Adele lay alone in the house, terrified as a torrent of fluids burst from her. She screamed, but no one heard her, and Oskar made his way into the world all on his own. When Chava finally came to the door and assessed the scene, she ran to fetch Golde the midwife who quickly and efficiently set Chava to boiling water and assembling clean cloths. Adele brought her babe to her breast and wished more than ever that Jonas was with her and that the three of them were in Vilna.

On a pretty day in November, a letter arrived from Jonas.

> *Dearest Adele,*
>
> *I am overwhelmed with joy upon receiving news of the birth of our son and only hope that he is doing well and that you are fully recovered from his birth. You will make such a good mother! I have settled nicely here in New York in a section called the Bronx. Wait until you see this city, so much bigger than Vilna even. I rent a tiny room so that I don't spend big money and will be able to bring you and Oskar here soon. Also, I am working with the immigration office to get your papers.*
>
> *All my love, Jonas.*

All through that bitter cold winter Adele kept Oskar and that letter close to her breast. Deep snows prevented the stage from making regular mail deliveries, but Adele was sure that once spring arrived, so would a letter beckoning her to New York City, the Bronx.

Papa loved his new grandson, worried over him. He began to caution Adele: "Even if he sends for you, your Jonas, how will you travel? It is too dangerous to go to any port on the Baltic, the Germans have troops all along there."

This could not be. After all this waiting, surely there would be a way for Adele and Oskar to go to America. *Send for us soon, Jonas!* she cried silently every cold dark night.

The snow was still deep when a rider delivered mail in the last days of March. As if Jonas had heard her father, he wrote—

> "*Even though President Wilson continues to declare neutrality, we receive reports here of the advances of German forces. I worry about your safety as you travel. Were I to be able to send for you—and I hope to within a few months—you may have to find a way to journey east through Asia rather than risk being detained by German troops.*"

Adele threw the letter to the floor in despair. "I should find a way? How can I do this? Why is my husband not here to care for his wife and child?" Oskar whimpered, frightened by his mother's outburst.

Chava took the baby from her sister. "You must be strong, Addie. It is hard, I know, but there must be some way. We'll ask Aleksandras, the stage driver, the next time he comes through. Come now, be brave for your boy's sake." She handed Oskar back to Adele and bent down to pick up the letter. "Jonas is too far away to know the best way for you to travel. We will figure this out, you and me."

Adele eyed her sister skeptically, but comforted Oskar, patting the baby on his back as she swung him side to side with her. "Do you think so, Chava? Aleksandras is not Jewish, is he?"

"He is a good man—we are only asking him for advice. We will find a way for you. Pay no attention to Papa. It will be as dangerous to stay here as to travel to America. You belong with your husband."

"But then what about you and Papa? Shouldn't you come, too?"

"As if!" shrugged Chava. "That's not about to happen."

Adele realized she had never totally appreciated her sister's strong will. She reached to hug her with her free arm. Chava allowed this for the briefest of moments, then pulled away.

"In the meantime, you had best be sure you are eating and sleeping well. You must build up your strength." She gave Adele a stern emphatic nod, then turned to the cookstove. "I will make us some barley soup—there is still a good bone."

The next week when the stage pulled in to town, Chava went to talk with Aleksandras. As Adele watched from the window, she saw that suddenly Chava grabbed Aleksandras by the elbow and directed him toward their house. Aleksandras hesitated, glanced around, but then came with her.

They burst through the door, Chava saying, "Sister! You must listen to Aleksandras."

He looked at her, at the baby in her arms, and shrugged. "If you really mean to leave the village, you should do so as soon as possible. German soldiers are advancing quickly. Our Russian troops are coming to prevent their progress. The battle could be here any day."

"But I am waiting word from my husband," protested Adele.

"You should not wait. You should be prepared to leave at any moment. When the war comes to this village, no resident of Kuzhi will be safe." He shook his head a bit. "Especially your people." He stopped, he had already said too much.

"She needs to get to America," Chava reminded him.

"Iŝ oro! The best you can do now is get out of Lithuania, out of Russia even. There may be some safe passage along the way. The Amir of Afghanistan maintains his neutrality."

"Afghanistan! Where in the world is Afghanistan?" exclaimed Adele.

"You will see much of the world on your journey, God willing," Aleksandras said. "I must go. But you must ready yourself. Get your things together. Your Leaving Day will arrive on a moment's notice."

He left hurriedly; the sisters stared at each other. Chava glanced to Adele's feet. "At least you have a pair of sturdy boots."

"Oh, Chava! Must I walk to America?"

"Better than to Siberia." They had both heard the stories of Jews made to walk thousands of miles from their villages to Siberia because of some transgression against the Russian tsar. "You must choose only the most essential things for you and Oskar—keep your burden as light as possible."

"I wish you and Papa could come with me!"

"Papa will never leave his beloved Kuzhi."

It was so. Jonas was determined to escape the uncertainties of life as a Jew threatened by the whims of the tsar, with opportunities few and humiliations constant. But Papa clung to his roots, to the place that had been the homeland for generations of his forebears. Adele knew she couldn't even suggest that Chava leave him behind—although she wished with all her heart she could have her strong sister with her on this journey.

Over the next few days, Adele began to assemble a few things in the satchel she would take. She shed brief bittersweet tears when she recalled how—early in their planning—she had told Jonas she wanted to pack all of her mother's good dishes and ship them to America so she would have something from home in her new life. Now, she wrapped a single saucer from that beautiful china, and with Chava's approval, wrapped a small blanket around the pair of silver candlesticks they lit on Shabbos Eve and placed these treasures in the bottom of the satchel.

But before Aleksandras came again on his regular stage-coach run, Russian soldiers marched in—some on horseback, others on foot, all heavily armed—with their rifles and bandoliers of bullets strapped menacingly to their chests. They set up a headquarters at Yoffe's house, hanging a banner from his roof and installing the commander of the regiment and a half-dozen men to bed down there, pushing Yoffe's own family to crowd in with his sister next door. The rest of the soldiers rode north of the village to set up camp.

On the morning of April 27, Papa came rushing into the house after visiting with Yoffe. "The Germans are coming closer. The Russians have given permission to all Jews to leave Kuzhi. Our neighbors are leaving."

"What does this mean?" Adele asked. "Are we to leave now? How will I get to America?"

Papa looked first to Adele then to Chava. He straightened his shoulders. "I am not leaving. This is my home, this belongs to me. You may do as you wish, but I am staying. Where else would I go? Why is one place safer than another?"

So they watched as the five other Jewish families loaded up two carts with all their belongings. Zikaras told Papa they would head east to a village where his cousin lived.

Papa went out to plant wheat. Chava swept the kitchen. Adele checked the contents of her valise.

That night, Adele was awakened by a thundering of horses' hooves. She snatched Oskar out of his basket and ran to the window. "Get back," shouted Papa. "It's the Germans! Get your coats and boots on, we must run!"

Chava was throwing clothes on over her nightdress and then grabbed Oskar. "You dress; I will wrap the baby for travel."

"Travel?" thought Adele. Now, in the middle of the night? As she pulled on her clothes she glimpsed flame bursting forth from Yoffe's house. She heard gunshots. Horses pounded by.

Papa peeked out the window. "The Russians have come from camp. We cannot go out now," he said. "We're safest here inside, out of the line of fire." The three adults huddled in the corner of the house away from any window, Adele shushing the baby as he whimpered, sensing their fright.

The battle raged on until Adele wondered when they would run out of bullets. Then, as dawn crept hesitantly over the scene, all was still.

Papa cautiously opened the door. The acrid smell of wet wood burning drifted in. With daylight, they could see that a couple of the houses had been set afire. Papa rushed to join a bucket brigade that formed from the creek to Yoffe's house and the one next door. Soon the flames were extinguished.

The banner the Russians had suspended from Yoffe's house hung to the ground, half-burned. Two soldiers attempted to salvage it and hang what was left upright. The German attack had been turned back by the Russian infantry camped outside town.

"We live another day," Papa said, when he returned. He sat down at the table and Chava brought him tea—a hot dark brew poured into a glass over a blob of jam. He stirred and sipped. "What can we do? There is nowhere for us to go that is safe. We must pray that this war will move on, pass us by, and in the meantime we must live our lives." He scooted his chair back and stood. "I have chores to do."

After he had gone out, Chava said to Adele, "Make sure your satchel is all packed. This is the day Aleksandras comes; perhaps he will have some news."

"Do you think he will come even now?"

"We can only hope."

Adele decided to wash herself and Oskar and dress them both in clean clothes as if they were about to embark on a trip. She was checking the contents of the satchel when again horses' hooves clattered into the village. Through the window, Chava and Adele saw a small Cossack regiment fall into formation in front of Yoffe's house. The commandant remained mounted, then moved his horse out in front of the troops. He began to bark out an announcement:

"Treason has been committed here. The enemy was hidden among you and given a signal by local residents when it might be safe to attack. All who were involved in this scandalous affair are ordered immediately to surrender to the military field court for betraying their country and treasonous activities against our army. The more influential residents will be exiled to Siberia."

Chava clutched Adele. "We know who they mean when they say 'influential residents.' More Jews will be marched off to Siberia."

"Where is Papa?" Adele went to another window to see where their father might be.

"He is here!" hissed Chava.

"Where?" Adele rushed to her sister's side, peering out the window for Papa.

"Aleksandras. Not Papa. Aleksandras is here." The stage had pulled up now, between their house and Yoffe's, and between their house and the soldiers. She pushed at Adele. "Get your things."

"Now?"

"Now. Now! Hurry!"

Quickly the sisters bundled up the baby, closed the satchel, then opened the door. Chava ventured out, seeing Aleksandras atop the stage. He nodded to Chava, who motioned for Adele. "Come. Come now!" she hissed. She stepped aside for Adele to move into the stage with Oskar in her arms, then shoved the satchel in behind her. She ducked back quickly into the house, then gave a small wave to her sister as Aleksandras gave a command to his horses. Adele shrank back into the shadows of the coach as far as she could.

"Halt!" the Russian commander shouted at Aleksandras.

"It's just the usual stage," said Yoffe, standing outside his house under the half-burned banner.

"Ah!" The commandant peered into the stage from atop his mount. Adele cowered further into her dark corner, praying Oskar would remain quiet.

The commandant hesitated, but he seemed not to see anything in the stage. He studied the driver—who did not look to be Jewish. After what seemed an eternity, he said "Proceed," to Aleksandras. With that, Yoffe gave a nonchalant wave to Aleksandras and the stage moved briskly forward, past the assembled regiment, out of Kuzhi.

Adele straightened up on the seat, peeked into the bundle of blankets at the sleeping Oskar and breathed again.

Aleksandras took her as far south as he dared, dropping her at the station in Radviliskis where she could get a train to Vilna. Many Jews were gathering in this city; with Oskar in her arms, she joined a group traveling through to Rumania.

Days later, Adele found herself in Constantinople amidst a throng of people, more than she had ever seen in her life. Most seemed to be Turks, but there were so many others—Greeks, Armenians, Europeans—a few Jews. She listened for Yiddish in the babel that filled the air, so many conversations in so many languages. She asked the way to the synagogue; there she connected with yet another group that would make their way by boat up the Bosphorus River then over the Black Sea to Trabzon, the Silk Road port at the eastern end of the sea.

And thus she traveled—sometimes with dozens of fellow Jews fleeing this war, sometimes only with Oskar, a hired guide, and her few possessions. Along the way, she bartered first one silver candlestick and then another for passage through dangerous territory. Often terrified, she used that terror to fuel her energy on long treks—some by rail, some in rickety native carts, some on foot. Then, finally, by Pacific Mail steamer from Hong Kong to San Francisco. America.

Although Jonas was not able to meet her in California, workers of the Hebrew Immigration Society greeted her when she stepped onshore. They helped her get her train ticket to New York and saw her safely on her way, notifying Jonas when he might expect his wife and child.

By August, Adele and Oskar were safe in the arms of Jonas in New York City the Bronx. Jonas had found a slightly larger apartment just a few blocks from the one room he had lived in while awaiting his family. She found the Bronx to be filled with people—like Constantinople and Hong Kong—but here most people spoke English, although there were many Jewish families in their neighborhood. Yiddish was spoken in the kosher butcher shop on the corner.

Adele also decided New York City was very warm. She shopped for lighter weight cotton dresses, took Oskar outside on the stoop to sit in the shade and hope for a breeze.

Each day she checked the mail, but did not hear from Papa and Chava although she had written to let them know she had arrived safely. Alas, the one saucer from her mother's good dishes had not survived intact. She saved the pieces—she would glue them back together someday soon.

Late in the month, the story was in *The Jewish Daily Forward*, the newspaper Jonas brought home from work:

> *The complete falsity of the communiques about the
> Jews in Kuzhi was demonstrated on the 19th and 20th
> of July in the Duma by deputies N. M. Fridman, N. S.
> Chkheidze and A. F. Kerensky.*
>
> *From the statement of N. M. Fridman: "... The
> announcement that, in the village of Kuzhi our unit
> suffered because of treachery by the Jews and the local
> Lithuanian population was plastered up in every city
> in the Russian Empire. Gentlemen, we have looked
> into the matter. Mr. Kerensky, member of the Duma,
> went there, and I also carried out an investigation and
> it turned out that nothing of the sort happened there.
> It turned out that there were no cellars there to hide
> German soldiers. There was one Jewish cellar about 4
> arshins long by 3 arshins wide and the depth of a man
> standing, and further, that all the misfortunes took
> place April 28th, while the Jews had left on the 27th.
> They left with the approval of the military leadership,
> with permission of the officers, they were let go, which
> of course they would not have been had they been guilty
> of anything. It is known that information about this is
> at the disposal of the Minister of Internal Affairs, and
> nevertheless, this slander has not yet been overturned."*
>
> *From the statement of N. S. Chkheidze: "The gov-
> ernment cannot not know that of 40 houses in Kuzhi
> there are only three Jewish houses, with a total of six
> Jewish families, who were, at the time described in the
> communiques of the Pravitelstvennyi Vestnik, not in
> Kuzhi, since they had already left the village out of fear*

about the enemy attack, and that among those arrested under suspicion of leading Germans into Kuzhi there was not one Jew, only Lithuanians, and that all those arrested were released because of completely unfounded accusations."

But what of Papa and Chava? Adele despaired, knowing only too well they had remained when the other Jews left. Part of her suspected they had done so in order for Adele and Oskar to make the connection needed with Aleksandras. Papa and Chava were no doubt accused of being spies, as they were the only Jews left in Kuzhi.

Were they being forced to march to Siberia? While Adele walked to the corner for brisket.

Or, had the Germans advanced to their village and taken prisoners? While Adele played with Oskar in the nearby park.

Perhaps the entire village had been burned to the ground as the Russians retreated before the German advance. And all the while Adele was safe in President Wilson's neutral America…in New York City the Bronx.

Ostersonntag

Here Vivian sat—grinding away at the starter, trying to get a spark. Again. And again. She was pretty sure the thugs in Maintenance gave her the crankiest garbage truck at Camp Grant just because she was female and short. There was one other female garbage truck driver, but she was taller and had bigger tits, which somehow made her seem a more capable driver. Of course she was a better driver—she got a better truck! It sure irked Vivian. She wasn't even halfway through her rounds down here by the hospital and still had to go by the prisoners' barracks.

And it was cold. March 1943 was going to go into the record books as one of the coldest ever. Snow was piled in dismal gray mounds all around the camp. The ground was still frozen solid so it was bumpy and rattled her around in the cab of the truck—when the truck worked. She rubbed her hands together and blew on them. Vivian was fed up with winter. And with the useless guard who accompanied her and her truck and the prisoner assigned to load garbage into the truck as they putzed along. Charles. Here he came now, looking irritated—like it's her fault the stupid truck wouldn't start.

"What's up?" Charles glared at her. "You're not gonna finish before dark at this rate."

"If we had some decent equipment around here, we'd have been done in time for you to have your afternoon nap," Vivian retorted. She took a swig of Coke out of the bottle she always had with her.

"How can you drink that stuff in this weather?"

"Hey, it keeps me going. Better than sneaking off for that gut-destroying stuff you keep in that flask of yours." Vivian had never been a coffee drinker—much to her mother's dismay. She started drinking Coca-Cola in the mornings when she was a kid and kept right on through the decades, so she was probably the only thirty-seven-year-old person on base—male or female—who kept a bottle of pop in the truck instead of a thermos of coffee. Or, as in the case of Charles, some cheap whiskey in a flask.

The prisoner walked around from the back of the truck with a questioning look on his face. He, too, probably wanted to finish before dark.

"*Was ist los?* What is happening?" The tall and blond German prisoner, somewhat gaunt but ridiculously cheerful, smiled up at Vivian in the cab. By and large, the prisoners at Camp Grant were not a threatening bunch—many were still recovering from fighting with Rommel in North Africa. Here, they were given the same accommodations as the U.S. servicemen, and as established by the Geneva Convention, fed the same meals. A new bunch had arrived just last month.

"Can't get it started." Vivian knew the prisoners understood some English, even if they didn't speak it much.

"I help?" He had worked with them before; Vivian thought his name might be Albert.

"Sure." Vivian glanced at Charles to let him know this was her decision, her truck, her work detail.

Albert went around to the front and lifted the hood on the truck, poked around a little, then came back to Vivian.

"Coca-Cola?"

What? Was the guy thirsty already? He hadn't done anything. She wasn't sure she'd understood him correctly.

"Coca-Cola." He must be an observant fellow, to have known she had a coke with her at all times. Was he a German spy?

What the heck—she handed him her precious bottle of pop.

He took it and returned to the front of the truck. Vivian couldn't quite see what he was doing from behind the wheel, so she scooted over to the passenger side to take a peek. It looked for all the world like this dumpkoff was pouring her Coke into the engine!

"Hey!" Vivian jumped out of the cab and strode right up to the German prisoner, who seemed much bigger now that she was standing right beside him. "What do you think you're doing?"

"Is okay." He smiled at her. He handed back her now half-empty bottle and pulled a rag out of the back pocket of his PW uniform, then proceeded to rub away at the battery posts of the engine. "*Versuch's jetzt.*" Albert motioned for her to get back in the truck.

She did, and turned the key. A little sputtering, and the motor turned over. Albert beamed and closed the hood on the truck. Charles looked a little dumbfounded—how was he to treat a prisoner who volunteered to fix their truck?

"Okay, then. Back to work?" He motioned for Albert to resume his position at the back of the truck, but Albert was already headed that way, grinning at Vivian as he passed her. And winking. He winked at her! At least, she thought that's what she saw. The nerve of that guy.

Vivian quickly put the truck in gear. A prisoner is still a prisoner, after all. Who does he think he is? She knew Charles hadn't seen that cheeky wink from Albert—if, indeed, that's what his name was. So she could either report it to Charles or just keep an eye on him herself. Probably she should just keep an eye on him.

The rest of the morning passed without incident with Vivian clinging to the wheel, as usual, to keep her feet within reach of the gas and the brake and the clutch, and the truck chugging along without a miss. Charles kept his M-1 slung over his shoulder as he sauntered along. The prisoner, whatever his name was, scrambled to keep up, tossing garbage into the truck as Vivian kept moving at just above the usual pace, trying to make up for lost time.

They stopped for lunch. Charles and the prisoner went off to their separate dining halls while Vivian parked the truck next to a grove of cedars near the prisoners' barracks, where they would be resuming their rounds. She rolled down the window a little to get a sweet whiff of the cedars, then opened the brown paper bag containing the peanut butter and jelly sandwich her mother had packed for her that morning. She took a big bite, enjoying the way the peanut butter seemed to coat the insides of her mouth before she took a swig of what was left in her bottle of Coke. She made her next bite smaller—she wanted the lone sandwich to last a while—and forced herself to slow down, to breathe in the cedar-scented air, and to look around. Vivian unbuttoned her winter coat. It was becoming a little more uncomfortable every year, as she continued to grow from pleasingly plump to somewhat more than that. Somewhere inside Vivian there was a slimmer, dark-haired beauty.

She wondered where in the prisoner barracks this genial garbage-man-turned-mechanic bunked. New wood barracks had been completed just before the first shipment of PWs arrived. There was a road that ran down the middle of the prisoners' barracks with housing for a thousand on each side, north and south. Many of the PWs were quite impressed with their new quarters—double-decker bunks with mattresses, sheets, blankets, pillows and pillowcases. In the German army they slept on straw sacks and covered up with rough blankets. So far, not a single one of them had tried to escape. According to Charles, they had it so much better here they figured it was a good place to be until the war was over.

Vivian shivered. It couldn't feel too good to be so far from home, fenced in with barbed wire and armed guards posted in tall watchtowers keeping an eye on you. Every morning, when Vivian came to work, she passed armed guards on the roads leading into Camp Grant.

But here came her prisoner, looking happy and recently-fed, with the big PW letters stamped on his olive-green uniform—which otherwise was the same uniform the regular army wore. He had a little book in his hand.

"You're early," she said.

"*Ja.*" He waved an arm toward the cedar trees and sniffed. "*Gut?* Is nice?"

"Yes, it does smell nice."

The prisoner held up his book—it was a German-English dictionary. "You help?" He motioned back and forth between them, as if to remind her that he had helped her by fixing the truck.

Vivian hesitated. She got down out of the truck to examine the dictionary and then handed it back to him. He was a very tall German prisoner. She smoothed the front of her tan dress, brushing lunch crumbs away, then buttoned up the front of her maroon winter coat over her bulky middle.

"Make me understand better, *Ja?*"

"First, tell me your name." If she had to report any funny business, at least she'd know who to report.

"I am Albert Meinert."

"I thought so; I thought your name was Albert."

"Now you tell."

"You want to know my name?" That made sense, actually. "My name is Vivian. Vivian Johnson."

"Is nice. Vivian. Nice name." Albert paused, looking at her expectantly. "You help, Vivian?"

"I'm not really a teacher." Although Vivian's father was Swedish, her mother had been born in Germany and came to the U.S. as a toddler years ago. So Vivian thought she might know some words—the words one might spit out when things weren't going well in the kitchen, for instance.

"Is okay. Just *hilf mir*, okay?"

"Alright." What could it hurt?

"*Danke*." Albert smiled happily and began to page through his dictionary. He stopped when he found the word he was looking for.

"*Stadt?* What is this town?" he gestured off toward Eleventh Street, the main road along the east edge of the camp.

"Rockford." Vivian knew that answer.

"Is your *Heimstadt?*"

"I don't know what that means—Heimstadt."

"You live?" Albert again waved toward Eleventh Street.

"Oh. Oh, yes. I've lived in Rockford all my life."

"Nice *Ort?*"

"Sure. I guess."

"You have *Mann?*"

Vivian was pretty sure she knew that word. "Nah. Just me and my mom and dad. My brother is in the Navy, somewhere in the Pacific."

Too much—Albert looked puzzled. Vivian reached over and took the dictionary from him, then turned to the English-to-German section. She found the word FATHER.

"*Vater*, see?" she pointed to the word. "Father. And…" the word for Mother was right there, too. "*Mutter*." The two were so intently huddled over the dictionary they didn't see Charles approach.

"What's this? Now you're a garbage truck driver *and* a teacher?" Charles snickered.

"What's it to yuh?" Vivian climbed back into the truck as Albert hastily tucked the dictionary inside the front of his uniform.

It was Saturday so Vivian had the next day off. She drove the garbage truck six days a week, never knowing which prisoner and which guard would be working with her. As she rode the bus home from camp, she wondered if Albert would be assigned to her on Monday, and if he'd bring his dictionary with him again.

Vivian lived with her parents in their bungalow near the Swedish-American Hospital, a ways down Eleventh Street from the camp. It took just under a half-hour for her bus ride; quicker if there weren't many people getting on and off. She had never lived anywhere else in all her thirty-seven years. Vivian had worked at the knitting factory until the war broke out and Camp Grant was resurrected, rebuilt and expanded from its WW1 incarnation. The wages were better—she was doing a man's job, after all—although Vivian thought it took more skill to operate the knitting machine than it did to drive a garbage truck. Somehow, she felt she was performing a little bit of patriotic duty to work at Camp Grant.

Vivian did not jump to enlist in the Women's Army Corps, although her brother Tom rushed to a recruiting office the day after Pearl Harbor was attacked. He'd been gone almost eight months now on his latest tour of duty and the family worried about him on a daily basis—out there in the wide Pacific, too close to Japan for comfort. She was keenly aware of how lonely soldiers and sailors could be when they were far from home, and even thought briefly about volunteering for the USO, but the USO seemed to be comprised of girls prettier than Vivian. It didn't matter what you looked like if you drove a garbage truck.

It was dark by the time the bus reached her stop, but lights glowed warmly from inside the half-dozen houses on the short walk along scrupulously cleared sidewalks to her home. As she went up the steps she could hear the music pouring forth. Saturday night meant the broadcast from the Metropolitan Opera in New York at full volume. Vivian didn't follow it anywhere near as closely as her parents did—she preferred the swing music of Benny Goodman. The Andrews Sisters were her favorites. But there was something reassuring about the early Saturday night ritual of listening to the music from the Met over dinner. Tonight there was one of her mother's best—creamy macaroni and cheese, with canned pears for dessert—accompanied by the dulcet tones of the announcer, Milton Cross, guiding them through "Pagliacci." None of them understood Italian, but nevertheless their hearts were torn as Canio demanded his wife tell him the name of her lover.

"Any cookies?" her father asked.

"You know we're giving up sweets for Lent," her mother responded.

"You're giving up sweets, not me. I'm not the religious zealot in this family."

"Then you will have to learn to bake cookies yourself." Vivian's mother wasn't really all that religious—she just clung to old traditions in these trying times. "Besides, sugar is very dear just now and it takes a lot of sugar to make cookies." Giving up sweets for six weeks was a practical way of dealing with wartime shortages.

Her father shot Vivian a look of resignation and pushed back a little from the table, but did not leave his chair. This was where he would sit and listen to the final minutes of "Pagliacci." As short and dark-haired as her mother was, Vivian's father was tall and blond—a typical Swede, if there was such a thing. He was a mostly contented man; it didn't bother him that his daughter was still unmarried, living at home. In fact, he kind of liked having her around. Vivian's mother, on the other hand, despaired of her daughter's advanced age and spinsterhood. She went so far as to suggest that maybe—after the war—they should check with the doctors. Her mother heard there may be a way to correct Vivian's lazy eye; her left eye sometimes seemed not to focus with the right eye. Vivian could tell people were not sure which eye to look at when they spoke with her.

"After the war, Mother? And when will that be? Let's face it--I'm not going to magically turn into Miss America anytime soon."

On Monday, when Vivian went back to work, a prisoner she had never seen before was assigned to her work detail, and Charles was once again her guard. She thought about asking this new fellow if he knew Albert, but then realized that probably wasn't a good idea.

"Wonder where our mechanic is today?" Charles asked, giving Vivian what he probably thought of as a knowing look. Yep, better she didn't ask about Albert at all.

During her lunch break, parked in her truck in the same grove of cedars, she rolled down the window again to breathe in their refreshing scent. The late winter sun struggled to send a glimmer through the heavy branches. Vivian sighed and wished she had a German-English dictionary so she could put this half-hour to good use. It would be handy to know a little German so she could communicate with any prisoner she happened to be working with, right?

On Tuesday morning, Vivian found herself at the bus stop so early that she caught the bus ahead of her usual one by about twenty minutes. When she arrived at camp noticeably early, Charles was there to observe this aberration.

"So, good morning, Teach." Charles accosted her before she could climb up into her truck. "Think your pupil will show up today?"

"Can it, Charles. It wouldn't hurt you to learn a few words of some other language." She refrained from advising him it would make him seem less like a hayseed.

"They're our *enemy*, lady." Charles leaned in to sneer in her face. "We're not supposed to make all nicey-nice with them."

"They seem pretty harmless behind those barbed wire fences."

"Shows you what you know…"

Their discussion was interrupted by the arrival of Tuesday's prisoner, ready to go to work.

"*Guten Morgen!*" Vivian sang out and quickly hoisted herself into the cab and started up the truck for another day. She decided arguing with Charles was fruitless and maybe even unwise. She was not going to allow his surliness to ruin her day. It was a little warmer this morning, so she cranked the window down an inch to let in some fresh air.

By noontime it was warm enough that Vivian rolled the window down all the way when she pulled into the cedar grove for lunch. She ate her sandwich and then got out to walk around a bit and give her legs a stretch.

"Hello?" she heard from the other side of the truck. And there was Albert, grinning at her with his dictionary in hand. She was a little surprised at how happy she was to see him.

"Hello." Vivian walked around to the back of the truck where garbage was piled in the front end, but the rear of the truck bed was still clear. She hopped up to sit there, her short legs dangling in mid-air. Albert didn't have to hop up at all, just sat where his rear end met the truck's. He looked at Vivian and then behind him to the garbage in the truck. "Ach!" Albert stood, motioned to a felled tree some distance from the truck, and helped Vivian down from her perch.

As Vivian arranged herself on the log, Albert paged through his book. He sat beside her and opened the dictionary to a page where the corner was turned down. He read, "How are you?"

"I am well; how are you?"

"*Gut.*" Then he quickly corrected himself, "Good."

"It's okay. *Gut.* You can teach me some German while I teach you some English." She felt compelled to point to herself and then to Albert and back again to herself.

He grinned. "*Ja.*"

"It's almost the same." Vivian smiled. "*Ja.* Yeah."

Albert nodded. Vivian looked around, not sure just when Charles or the other prisoner would return. "Where are you working today?" she asked.

"Laundry—*ich arbeite* in Laundry."

"Ah."

Albert paged through his dictionary. "*Morgen?* Tomorrow I work garbage?

"That would be good." Vivian smiled and nodded somewhat vigorously, feeling a little foolish about the way she needed to reinforce her speaking with physical indicators.

"Yeah. Good." Albert nodded, too.

Vivian looked around, then waved her hand at the cedar grove.

"Trees," she said.

"Ah! Good *Geruch*," Albert waved at the trees, then poked Vivian on the shoulder. "Good trees, also."

"No, no." She laughed. "I am not a tree. Here, let me see." She took the dictionary from him, found the word for TREE. "*Baum*. Tree."

"Oh, *Baum*. Tree?" He looked embarrassed. "You not TREE. No." He looked puzzled. "What is…?" He pinched his nose.

For a minute, Vivian thought he wanted to know the word for NOSE, but then realized he wanted the word for SMELL. "Smell. Trees *smell* good."

"Ah! Trees smell good." He was delighted when she nodded her approval. "You, Vivian smell good," he declared.

She blushed, and then quickly pointed over to the bags of garbage in the truck. "Smell bad. Garbage smells bad."

"Smell bad," her student repeated after her. Vivian saw, beneath the branches, a pair of boots walking toward them out on the road. She jumped up and hastily pulled Albert to his feet.

"Time to get back to work," she said, pointing him in the direction from which he had come. He understood, tucked his book away and was off through the grove of trees.

Vivian was back in the cab of her truck by the time Charles and the other prisoner came into full view; she quickly started up the engine to avoid any conversation. She was pretty sure Charles had not seen Albert because he said nothing, just gave her a little mock salute before he headed to the back so he could keep an eye on the prisoner.

Albert was again assigned to her garbage detail the next morning. And there was a different guard walking alongside Albert.

"Good morning! I'm Thomas McGinty, and this dangerous man here is Albert." He smiled to let her know this was a joke.

"Ah, good. Glad to have your company, Thomas. But Albert has worked this detail a couple of times before—and he doesn't seem very dangerous." Vivian glanced quickly at Albert, who was standing behind the guard and grinning broadly.

"Just the same, I'll keep an eye on him for you."

"Thanks." Vivian was careful not to look again at the grinning Albert.

And so, when lunchtime rolled around, Thomas and Albert set off in the direction of their dining halls and Vivian pulled into the cedar grove. She had finished only half her sandwich before Albert returned, holding the dictionary out in front of him to signal it was time for another lesson. Vivian got down out of the cab and the two of them headed to their log bench. Albert sat with his long legs folded up in front of him.

"Did you even eat any lunch?" she asked.

"*Nein.*" He waggled the dictionary at her.

"But you need to eat." She looked at his thin frame. "You need to rebuild your strength." She reached into her paper bag. "Here, you can have the other half of my sandwich."

Albert seemed about to protest, but then accepted the sandwich and took a generous bite. She smiled, nodding her head. Then Albert offered the sandwich back to her.

"Oh, no. You eat it. It's yours. Sorry it isn't more."

But Albert wasn't having it. "You eat." He moved the sandwich back and forth between them. "We *teilen.* We eat." He held the rest of the sandwich up to her mouth so she could take another bite. Without looking at him, she took as small a bite as she could, then pushed his hand back. Albert finished off the sandwich in a single bite.

"Ah! Now?" He held up his dictionary.

For the next few weeks, Vivian persuaded her mother to make two peanut butter and jelly sandwiches. "What do you need two sandwiches for? You don't look like you're starving to death."

"I can make them myself, if you want," Vivian offered, ignoring her mother's pointed remark.

"I'll make them." And so her mother did; and when someone other than Albert showed up for garbage detail, Vivian gave the extra sandwich to either that prisoner or the guard, depending on who looked hungriest.

March warmed into April with Albert making great progress in his English, and Vivian learning some German along the way. Mostly, she insisted on all-English conversation.

"How old are you?" she asked, using a lesson in NUMBERS to answer a question that had been niggling at her thoughts.

Albert ran a finger down the dictionary's page. "I twenty-seven." He beamed at her.

Vivian was shocked. She definitely thought he was older, closer to her own age. Must be the ravages of war.

"How old are you?"

"You're never supposed to ask a lady her age."

"Ach!" He waved his hand dismissively. "How old?" She noticed Albert had figured out her lazy eye problem—he just concentrated on her right eye.

"Thirty-seven."

His grin turned mischievous. "Is nice—thirty-seven."

They had already been through the pages about FAMILY so Vivian knew that Albert had a mother and father back in Germany and three sisters. No brothers. No wife.

"I thought you were older."

"I have birthday soon," he said, as if that would make up the difference.

"Really? When is your birthday?"

"*am fünfundzwanzigsten*." He riffled through the dictionary, then stabbed a page. "April twenty-five."

"Oh, that is soon. And it's Easter Sunday."

"*Ostersonntag*? Really?"

"Yes, Easter is April twenty-fifth this year. Late."

"I be *Oster hase*." He laughed at her quizzical expression. More paging through the book, which was becoming quite beat-up by now. "Ah! Easter Bunny!"

"You'd be a pretty big bunny. Do they have Easter Bunny in Germany?"

"We first, before you Yanks."

"Really? So we stole it?"

"It's okay. We share." Sharing seemed to be one of Albert's favorite things. Albert paged again through the dictionary.

"At my home, before the war, we have birthday cake with candles. You do this?"

"Even now, we do that."

"Really? I wish…" Before he could put his wish into English, they heard Charles making his return and the lesson was over.

Weeks later, Vivian would wonder what prompted her to ask her father if she could take the family car to camp on Saturday.

"What, the bus isn't good enough?"

"Sure it is. But the car just sits here on Saturdays—why can't I take it to work?"

"Okay." Her dad was a pushover.

Her mother, on the other hand: "What if I have to go to the grocery store?" Her mother never drove, she just walked two blocks down to the corner Piggly Wiggly.

"I can take you when I get home from work."

Her mother eyed her skeptically, but it was decided.

So, on a pretty second Saturday in April, Vivian drove through the gate at Camp Grant in her father's '37 Ford sedan. She waved at the guard, who smiled and raised his eyebrows— recognizing her upgrade in transportation.

She parked near the maintenance shed where the garbage trucks were kept and waited a few minutes to see if Albert would show up so she could show him the car. Sure enough, just as she was about to give up and hoist herself into the garbage truck, Albert appeared.

"I drove my father's car to work today." Vivian pointed proudly at the gleaming sedan parked just feet away. Albert's eyes widened.

"Vater's? Yes?" He grinned at her. "You drive?"

"Yes, I drive. If I can drive this garbage truck, I can certainly drive a '37 Ford." She started to open the truck's door and Albert moved quickly to open it for her.

"Is good. Your father's car is good."

"Right." Vivian had expected Albert to be impressed but she was tickled with his unexpected enthusiasm.

At dinner that early evening, mock chicken legs were accompanied by the strains of "Tristan und Isolde" from the Met.

Vivian glanced at her mom. "This is a German opera, right?"

"My favorite Wagner." Her mother nodded happily.

"Back then, Germans were the good guys," her father pointed out.

"Ach! Don't talk about it." Her mother stood and began clearing the table.

"Not all Germans are evil. Some are even risking their lives to help the Jews." Her father handed her his empty plate.

"Mostly they are idiots falling all over themselves in goose-stepping obedience to that murderer!" Her mother's face was flushed as she grabbed a handful of silver from the table.

"Some of the prisoners at camp are really helpful." Vivian spoke carefully.

"Any cookies?" her father looked from Vivian to the cookie jar.

"Easter is in two weeks," his wife said.

"Thank God for the risen Lord!"

"Karl! *Du sollst dich schämen!*"

"What? I'm not mocking. I'm just eager to have a little something sweet again."

"Soon enough." His wife moved to take the last of the dinnerware into the kitchen.

"You sit, Mom. I'll do the dishes." Her mother looked at Vivian in wonder. "It's okay—since I didn't have to waste all that time riding the bus today, I'm not as tired. You made dinner, I'll do the cleaning up."

"Sit, Hilda. Enjoy the Wagner." Her father motioned to her chair at the table, and somewhat hesitantly, her mother sat.

On Thursday noon as they sat secluded in their grove, Albert asked if Vivian would be driving her father's car again on Saturday.

"Yes, I think so. Unless something comes up and he needs the car himself."

"That would be too bad."

"Well, it's not likely. I'll probably be able to drive it again this Saturday."

Albert hesitated. "I should like someday to take a ride in an automobile such as this."

Vivian smiled at him. "Maybe someday. Maybe when this war is over we can all go wherever we want, with whomever we want."

He nodded. "Yes, maybe. And maybe someday we celebrate birthdays again." Albert gave her a long doubtful look.

On the next Saturday, amidst Ezio Pinza's singing of *Figaro*, Vivian asked—as casually as possible—"Would it be okay if I invite one of the fellas from camp for next weekend?"

Her father put down his silverware to hear the rest of this; her mother gripped hers tightly, eyes wide.

"It just so happens it's his birthday on Easter Sunday, and he's homesick, and I just thought it would be nice to give him a weekend away from camp." Vivian paused. "He could stay in Tommy's room."

"You mean have him stay overnight?" her father asked.

"It would be easier if I just brought him home with me after my shift on Saturday." Vivian hoped this sounded as logical as she planned.

"This is a young man who…who is a friend of yours?" Her mother smiled hesitantly, not quite believing what she was hearing.

"I've made some friends at camp, yes."

Her father looked at her mother. "Why wouldn't she?"

"It's just…" her mother paused.

"Well, would it be all right then?"

"I think it's a great idea. Especially with Tom gone—we'll be entertaining a service member in his place," her father said.

Vivian tried not to cringe. Now was not the time to tell them of Albert's true status at camp.

"We'll have a wonderful Easter celebration," her mother clapped her hands in excitement. "I'll order a leg of lamb from the butcher."

Vivian told Albert of her plan as they shared peanut butter and jelly sandwiches Monday noon. His eyes widened.

"*Ernst?*" He jumped to his feet from their cedar log. "This is possible?"

"We will make it possible. I thought about asking for permission…"

"Nein! Permission never happen!"

"That's what I thought. I'm not sure they would allow it. So…I'll bring you some of my brother's clothes and we'll drive out of here with you dressed as a civilian. It should work."

Albert looked at her approvingly. She was relieved he didn't think her plan too risky. He pulled her to her feet. "You are *wunderbar*." He fumbled for the word—"Amazing!"

"It'll be your birthday present," she said, trying to make it sound as if it was no big deal.

"Ah, yes! Birthday. *Ostersonntag*. Easter."

"Shhh." Vivian glanced around. "Nobody must know. Nobody must even suspect."

He nodded. "Nobody must know."

"Now, if for some reason you are not assigned to garbage detail the rest of the week, this is where we will meet at the end of the work day on Saturday. I'll wait for you here with my father's car. Understand?"

"Your father's *wagen?*"

"You saw it—the gray '37 Ford." She realized how silly this information was—there would be no other civilian vehicle parked in this grove. "Okay?"

"Okay." Albert grabbed her into an impulsive hug.

Vivian almost melted into his joyful embrace. Almost. She stepped back quickly. "Not here."

Albert looked around. "Okay. Yes."

At the end of her shift on Saturday, she pulled the garbage truck into the maintenance yard and then went over to the Ford, backed it out of the parking place, and headed for the cedar grove instead of going right to the exit. This was the first part Vivian was worried about. But nobody stopped her, nobody asked her where she was going. So far, so good.

Soon enough, Albert came down the road. She could see the bottom of his legs through the trees and recognized his cadence. She realized he was trying to be nonchalant, unhurried. But as soon as he was in the grove, he rushed over to her.

"Is okay?" he asked.

"I think we're good." She handed him the bundle of her brother's clothes. "You can change in the car. I'll watch to be sure nobody comes."

Albert nodded and got into the roomy sedan. Vivian turned her back to the car and kept an eye on the road that edged the grove. She could hear Albert bumping around and imagined him removing his "PW" uniform, then pulling on Tommy's shirt and trousers. Fortunately, they were about the same build. She heard the car door open.

"I am G. I.?" Albert asked.

Vivian smiled. The shirt sleeves of the light blue cotton shirt ended two inches above his wristbone and the dark gray trousers were really short. "You are a tall person. That's what you are, tall."

He shrugged helplessly.

"Never mind. No one will be able to tell when you're in the car."

"Yes." Albert nodded.

And no one did. It went more smoothly than Vivian could have imagined—mostly because the person on guard duty as they drove out of camp was somebody different and he didn't question Vivian driving out with some civilian in the passenger seat.

She breathed a huge sigh of relief. The first part had gone exactly according to plan.

When they walked in the front door, Vivian realized her mother had gone all out to prepare a welcome for their visitor. A fire was in the fireplace in the living room, the fragrance of sausages cooking made its way from the kitchen, and she could see into the dining room that the table was set with the good dishes. What was her mother going to do to top this tomorrow, for Easter Sunday, she wondered?

Her father rose to greet them.

"Dad, this is Albert. Albert, this is my father."

Albert extended his hand and said carefully, "How do you do?"

Her father glanced at Vivian, shook Albert's hand, and said, "Welcome." He paused, looked again at Vivian, then back to Albert. "Welcome to our home, Albert."

Vivian's mother rushed in from the kitchen, beaming. "Hello, hello! Welcome!" She rushed forward to shake Albert's hand.

"And this is my mother. Mom, this is Albert."

"How do you do?" Albert said.

Her mother stopped, looked him up and down, looked over to Vivian. She took her hand away, tucked it securely inside her left hand and retreated a step. Then another.

"I am so happy to be here," Albert said. Even Vivian realized there was a distinct German accent to his much-practiced phrase. Albert smiled at Vivian's mother, who looked ever more confused.

Her father stepped forward. "And we are happy to have you." He motioned to a chair by the fireplace, next to his. "Here, sit here, Albert." Then turned to his wife, "Supper will be ready soon, right, Hilda?"

"*Ja.*" Vivian's mother recovered her voice, and her response came out in German. Her face reddened. "It's all ready. We can eat now." She hurried to her kitchen. When Albert, Vivian and her father were seated at the dining room table, she brought in a platter of sausages and one of potato pancakes.

Albert beamed. "Ah! Beautiful!" he said as her father passed him the sausages.

Her mother eyed him carefully. "There's applesauce." She handed him the bowl. "Homemade," she added.

"So good! All my favorites!"

By chance, Vivian's mother was serving a typical German supper. "This is one of our favorite Saturday night meals," explained Vivian's father. "My wife is a good cook."

"Yes. Very good." He flashed her mother that engaging smile. Vivian saw her mother struggle—not sure how to react.

"So, Albert—is it really your birthday tomorrow?" Her mother was going to determine what was real in this bizarre set of circumstances.

"Yes, April twenty-fifth. That is my birthday. Sometimes comes on Easter, like this year."

"Makes for quite a celebration," her father observed.

"Yes. Happy birthday with lamb cake." Albert was clearly enjoying himself—he was the most relaxed person in the room—happily consuming his sausages and potato pancakes with gusto.

After Albert had seconds, and the rest of them had finished their meal, Vivian's mother rose and said, "Vivian, will you help me clear things?"

Before she could even reply, Albert jumped to his feet.

"Yes. I help." He picked up his plate and her father's and followed Vivian and her mother into the kitchen.

"Thank you, Albert. And now, if you will take coffee to Mr. Johnson."

The minute Albert left the kitchen, her mother turned on Vivian. "Those are Tommy's clothes! This man is not an American G. I., is he, Vivian?"

Vivian almost imperceptibly shook her head 'no.'

"He's a prisoner of war, isn't he? You've brought a PRIS-ONER into our home?!"

"But see how nice he is, Mom?"

Just then Albert reappeared. "Mr. Johnson wants sugar. *Kaffeesahne*. Cream," he corrected—and glanced guiltily at Vivian.

"Here." Vivian's mother handed him the sugar. "*Zucker*." And the cream, "*Kaffeesahne*."

Albert smiled at her, then at Vivian, and back to her mother. He has been recognized and was being welcomed in his native tongue. Vivian held her breath.

"*Danke*," Albert said.

"*Bitte*," her mother replied.

Albert went back into the dining room, cream and sugar in hand. Vivian dared to look at her mother, who returned Vivian's gaze and—shrugged her shoulders. "You have made a very big mistake, Vivian. But I don't know what we can do about it at this moment. He is who he is." She shook her head in bewilderment. "A very big mistake."

When coffee was over, Vivian's mother stood and announced: "I am going to dye some eggs now. I have them all hard-boiled. Anyone want to help?"

Albert looked at her questioningly.

"*Wir bemalen Ostereier,*" she explained.

"Ah! Yes. I help."

"Me, too." Vivian said.

"I think I'll finish reading the paper," her father said.

"Put on the Victrola, why don't you, Karl?" Vivian's mother requested.

Soon, the egg-dying trio was at its task in the kitchen accompanied by the familiar strains of *Tristan and Isolde*. Albert hummed along, occasionally singing the words softly. Vivian's mother watched him, looked away when she realized Vivian was watching her.

Eventually the eggs were dyed. Albert yawned broadly. "So much *Aufregung,*" he said. "I am tired. I go to bed now?"

"Oh, okay." Vivian hated for the evening to end.

"Here, I'll show you Tommy's room," her mother said.

While her mother showed Albert the room and where the bathroom was, and gave him a set of towels, Vivian stepped out onto the front porch. It was dark, with what was left of the waning moon affording a minimum of silver sheen. Albert had gone off to bed so early—she had hoped they would have some time together after her parents went to bed, although she suspected they would have stayed up as long as it took to outlast her. She would have to take Albert back to Camp Grant after dinner tomorrow, while the car was still available. She couldn't risk taking him on the bus Monday morning—and besides, his absence would assuredly be discovered by then. Maybe it already had. What would become of him? Of *them?*

The next morning, Vivian was up early, tiptoeing around the kitchen, making coffee. The brightly-dyed eggs sat in a bowl on the counter. Soon her parents were up, and the three of them sat at the dining room table, quietly drinking coffee.

There was no sound from Tommy's room. Albert must have been sleeping soundly, dreaming of Easter dinner, perhaps.

An hour passed. Their quiet conversation grew a little louder. Still no noises of movement, or even a trip to the bathroom.

"I hope he's alright," Vivian's mother said.

"Should I check?" her father asked.

"Oh, let him sleep," Vivian decided.

Another half-hour passed. Coffee was finished, dishes in the sink. Vivian's father made a pretense of reading the paper and finally put it down, stood up, and without consulting Vivian, went to knock on Tommy's door. There was no response.

"Albert?" he said. Nothing.

Vivian's father opened the door. He took a quick look in, then pushed the door wide open. From the hall where they had been watching, Vivian and her mother could plainly see a bed that appeared not to have been slept in. Her father stepped inside, looked around, then re-emerged.

"He's not here. It looks as if he has left."

"He's gone?" Vivian rushed into the room in disbelief. The room was cold, a window wide open. She stood there, looking around as if Albert might materialize. She looked at her father and past him to her mother. "He's gone."

Monday noon when Charles and some new prisoner went off to lunch and Vivian pulled her garbage truck into the cedar grove, she looked around, half expecting to see Albert wander toward her, waving his dictionary. But there was no Albert. He hadn't even said "*auf wiedersehen.*" She cranked the window down. The sweet smell of the cedars turned her stomach.

The Good Dishes

Felicity could hear Mom hissing at Cassandra in the middle of the dark night. "Do you think I don't know what you're doing—parked out there in the driveway in that boy's car 'til all hours of the night?"

Felicity crept down the stairs to see Cassandra get bawled out again. Her older sister wasn't much for curfews. But this time Mom really lost it. She was armed with a yardstick and started smacking Cassandra on the backs of her bare legs. "What do I have to do to make you behave yourself?" Mom pleaded, vexed beyond belief, but trying not to yell for fear of waking her other two daughters.

Isabelle quietly came to the top of the stairs. "Felicity, get back to bed. This is none of our business."

Felicity ignored her middle sister and continued to sit, halfway down the stairs, alarmed and yet fascinated with this version of their normally unperturbed mother.

"Felicity…" Isabelle implored.

Reluctantly, Felicity crept back up the stairs. All three girls slept in the bungalow's attic space that had been converted into one big bedroom; Cassandra would have to come upstairs soon.

"What were you doing?" Felicity insisted, the moment Cassandra's shadowy form appeared at the top of the stairs.

"Nothing. Talking." You could tell she was smirking, even in the dark.

"Go back to sleep, Felicity. It's a school night," said Isabelle, her voice muffled as she pulled her covers up over her head, wanting to be done with the incident.

When Dad left Mom for that floozie Monica, Cassandra was quite taken with the idea that their father would be that daring.

She viewed her father's infidelity as behavior in accord with the times; if Eddie Fisher—over whom Cassandra swooned—could leave that pretty little Debbie Reynolds for the seductress Elizabeth Taylor, then it made sense that Dad would leave Mom for Monica, the office temptress.

Isabelle, on the other hand, was a fan of the safe and sane Perry Como. She wept in sympathy for her mother.

Felicity wondered if she would still be able to go to Brownies because Dad left with their only car. How would she get home from Brownie meetings? Tuesday was her favorite day of the week because that's when she wore her Brownie uniform to school—a neatly tailored little dress that said she belonged. With a name like Felicity, she needed all the help she could get.

Their mother loved romance novels; she squirreled them away so their impressionable young minds wouldn't be tainted by the bodice-ripping described in their pages, but they were definitely where she went to escape the real world—had been for years. Hence her daughters' names: Cassandra, Isabelle and Felicity.

Felicity's biggest concern was relieved when Mom said she was old enough to walk home by herself from Brownies. The school was only ten blocks away and even in winter it was barely starting to get dark by the time she got home on Tuesdays.

Cassandra was responsible for fixing supper on the nights when Mom worked and she always had it ready when Felicity walked in the door. Tonight it was macaroni-and-cheese, again.

"Maybe we could have some salad or a vegetable with it?" Isabelle suggested.

"You can fix it if you want," Cassandra granted her permission while busily scarfing down her plateful.

"I'm fine with mac 'n cheese," Felicity said.

"Maybe we could have some fruit for dessert?" Isabelle bargained.

"I'm going over to Sharon's," Cassandra informed them, pushing back her chair and heading into the kitchen to dump her plate in the sink.

Isabelle and Felicity were responsible for clean-up.

"Don't you have any homework?" Isabelle asked as Cassandra pulled on her sweater.

"All done." Of course it was. Cassandra always got most of her homework done while the others were diddling around in class. She got straight A's without half trying, even though she was in the more difficult honors classes. Which made it tough on Isabelle coming along behind her as a sophomore and having all the teachers greeting her with "Oh! You're Cassandra's sister!"

Isabelle's one superior quality was her hair. While both Cassandra and Isabelle had just regular light brown hair, Isabelle's was naturally curly and Cassandra's was straight as a stick. Isabelle could step out of the shower and run her fingers through her short-cropped curls and look presentable; Cassandra slept in pin curls every night.

Felicity wore pigtails and was glad there was a big gap between Cassandra and Isabelle and her; Felicity was in fourth grade. The high school teachers might have forgotten all about Cassandra and her straight A's by the time Felicity arrived.

Isabelle washed and Felicity dried. "At Connie's house, her dad always helps with the dishes," Felicity observed.

"That's the kind of husband I'm going to have," Isabelle stated.

"Did our dad ever help with the dishes?"

"When Mom was in the hospital having you, he fixed supper and cleaned up and everything." Isabelle swallowed. "But that's the only time I remember."

"Is that why they got divorced?"

Isabelle looked at her younger sister, considering. "I guess that probably had something to do with it."

"Maybe if I knew how to do the dishes then, they wouldn't have had to get divorced."

"Oh, I don't think so!" Isabelle leaned over a little to look her sister in the eye. "I don't think there's anything we could have done. It was just something that happened."

"But don't you miss Dad?"

"A little, but probably not as much as you do. You were… you are his favorite."

"You really think so?" Felicity was genuinely surprised.

"Oh, I know so." Isabelle bit her tongue in time to avoid adding the part about Cassandra being such a handful she drove her dad crazy, and Isabelle too close behind to provide much relief, even though she did her best to always be a good girl. Felicity was younger enough that she was the joyful diversion that sometimes saved a troubled marriage—just not this one.

"Is it because I look like Dad?" Felicity asked.

"Well, you do have his red hair—but other than that, I think you look more like Aunt Carol than Dad." Isabelle might have been stretching the truth a bit here.

"Maybe I'll be tall like Aunt Carol."

"You've got a good start!" Isabelle smiled at her younger sister—who, although only ten, was nearly as tall as her older siblings.

The girls finished up with the dishes—an array of mismatched pieces from various sets that were onetime whole, with replacement cups and plates obtained when the A&P ran those specials where you received a free piece of china with the purchase of $25 worth of groceries.

"Well, I *do* have homework," Isabelle said, reaching into the stack of books she had piled on the dining room buffet. "What about you?" She took her math book to the oblong dining room table covered in a beige plastic cloth.

"No, I don't have any tonight." Felicity was happy fifth grade wasn't as hard as high school. "Can I turn on the TV?"

"Alright, but keep the volume down."

"Okay." Felicity plunked down on the faded green living room couch and was delighted to discover it was still early enough for the second half of *"Name That Tune."* Her mom came home during the *"Phil Silvers Show"* that followed, bringing leftovers from the donut shop where she worked.

"I'm glad that you work at the donut shop," Felicity told her mom, peering into the bag to choose from the half-dozen sugary and fragrant assortment.

"I'm glad you're glad." Her mom gave her a hug. "But eat your donut at the table, okay? And after you finish, you'd better brush your teeth and get to bed." She pulled a paper napkin from the plastic holder that sat on the table and put it in front of the chair that Felicity was about to sit down in. "What about you, Isabelle? Want a donut?"

"Are there any cinnamon and sugar ones?"

"Two…lucky you!"

"What about Cassandra?"

Her mom admired Isabelle's innate generosity. Where did that come from? "Cassandra likes the glazed, there's one of those, too. Don't worry about her, Cassandra will have to take what's left whenever she gets home."

And again that night, Cassandra came creeping in the dark house well past her curfew, but their mom was too tired to get up and argue with her about it and simply turned over in her bed, letting her vexatious daughter think she was asleep.

Later that same week, when they all sat down to supper together on Thursday, their mom's night off, Cassandra surprised everybody by announcing, "I've got a new job! I start work Saturday at W. T. Grant!" She beamed with pride.

"But what about your job at the library?" her mom asked.

"I'll make ten cents more an hour at Grant's," Cassandra said, "AND I get an employee discount!" She reached for the meatloaf and slid a piece onto her plate. "Besides, it'll be a lot more fun than working with those two old biddies at Southeast Branch."

"It's liable to be a lot more work," her mom cautioned. "What will you be doing? Clerking?"

"To start with, I'll be stocking shelves. Then I'll move up to clerking," Cassandra assured her mother.

"And how will you get to work?"

"On the bus, same as for the library. I'll transfer at 7th Street to get the bus downtown."

"Well, you seem to have this all figured out…"

"Yep. It's going to be a fun job, and I'll be downtown where all the other stores are."

Her mom figured Cassandra's paychecks would likely be spent before they were barely in her pocket.

The new job meant Cassandra acquired yet another new boyfriend, someone named "Chuck," who was already out of high school, and was training to be an assistant manager at Grant's. All of this information was breathlessly revealed at supper only one week after Cassandra began stocking shelves. Chuck had a car, so he conveniently provided a ride home for Cassandra; some days he worked an earlier shift and then had to go back to the store later to give Cassandra her ride home.

"Isn't he sweet?" Cassandra observed as she shared Tuesday supper with her sisters when she had the night off.

"Does Mom know that you're not taking the bus home?" Isabelle asked.

"What difference does it make?" Cassandra pushed back her chair, ready to hurry off somewhere. "It saves me busfare. Anyway, it's not a secret. You can tell her, if you want."

"How old is Chuck?" Felicity wanted to know. She thought you had to be pretty old to be an Assistant Manager.

"He's twenty-one. An adult."

"Isn't that kind of old for you?" Isabelle asked the question she was sure her mother would have asked, had she been there.

"Not really. He's barely five years older than me, closer to four, actually." Cassandra dumped her dish and silverware into the sink. "Look at Aunt Carol—she's seven years younger than Uncle Tony."

"Are you gonna get married?" Felicity asked, her eyes widening.

"No, silly. I was using them as an example. I still have to finish high school."

"And go to college," Isabelle intervened.

"Well, maybe." Cassandra shrugged into her cardigan.

"As smart as you are? Why wouldn't you go to college?" Isabelle wondered.

"Well, look at Chuck. He didn't go to college and he's already almost an assistant manager."

"But.." Isabelle started to point out that Cassandra had always said she wanted to be a teacher.

"I have to run. Sharon and I are working on a Biology project." And with that, Cassandra was out the door, leaving Isabelle and Felicity alone at the dining room table.

"Does Mom know Cassandra isn't going to college?" Felicity asked.

"MAYBE she isn't. Things could change by next week, you know how Cassandra is."

"Okay." Felicity figured Isabelle might be right, but maybe not. And she was already counting on being able to move into the dormer space that Cassandra occupied in their attic bedroom so she'd have the next best thing to a room of her own. Currently, Isabelle and Felicity had twin beds in the large open space at the head of the stairs. She assumed Cassandra would go off to college, probably Northern Illinois University close by, and would live on campus, freeing up that coveted dormer space. This was not good news.

Isabelle faced her own quandary. Should she tell her mother about this conversation? Would that be 'tattling,' or something else Cassandra wouldn't care if she told their mother? Maybe this would give Mom more to worry about. Why do I have to worry about this stuff? Isabelle wondered.

As they were finishing supper a few weeks later, Cassandra leaned over her plate and asked in hushed tones—"How would you two like to help me with a surprise for Mom?" The hushed tones really weren't necessary since their mother was at the donut shop, a twenty-minute bus ride away, but Cassandra was all about drama.

"A surprise?" Felicity was excited.

"What kind of a surprise?" Isabelle asked.

"You'll see. And you'll get to meet Chuck, too. He'll be here any minute with the surprise. It's something I got at work and he's delivering it for me."

Sure enough, while the girls were clearing the table a knock came at the back door which led into the kitchen.

Cassandra rushed to hold the door open as Chuck entered carrying a large brown cardboard box that was obviously heavy. He even staggered a little making his way to the counter to deposit the box in the first available open space. Fortunately, it wasn't a long distance from door to counter—Chuck was not a big person.

"What is it?" Felicity exclaimed. "It's such a big box!"

"You must be Chuck," Isabelle said, somewhat shyly. Then she stuck out her hand in her most grownup manner.

"Yes," he seemed embarrassed—not the swaggering Assistant Manager Person Isabelle had been expecting.

"This is Isabelle…and this is Felicity." Cassandra performed the perfunctory introductions. "This is Chuck." She laid her hand on his shoulder in a proprietary manner.

"Hi," he said. "Nice to meet you." He turned to Cassandra somewhat apologetically. "Sorry I can't stay and help you but I have to get back to the store. I'm on my supper hour."

"Oh, right," Cassandra remembered then—the extra effort he had made on her behalf. "Thanks. Appreciate it." She walked him back over to the door and gave him a quick smooch on the cheek. "See you tomorrow night."

Felicity stared. It was the first time she had seen her sister kiss a boy. Isabelle looked at Cassandra with new-found respect—it was clear her sister was in charge in her relationship with this "older man."

Cassandra was busy opening the box, tearing at the tape with a scissors from the junk drawer. She pulled rumpled brown packing paper out and then held aloft a pretty china cup—white, painted with a delicate pink rose.

"Aren't they pretty?" Cassandra beamed. "It's a whole set of cups and saucers and plates—all matching. Enough for four people."

"Are they for us?" Felicity asked.

"Sure thing! Well, for Mom, mostly."

"Did you buy these yourself?" Isabelle wanted to know, reaching in and pulling out the matching saucer.

Cassandra nodded. "I used practically all of my first two paychecks. The minute I saw them that first week when I was shelving—I knew I wanted Mom to have them. A whole set of matching dishes."

"They're really pretty," Felicity agreed. "We can use them when we have company."

"No!" Cassandra was decisive. "These are for everyday. We are going to have good dishes that match whenever we sit down for breakfast or lunch or supper."

"Where will we put them?" Isabelle wondered, glancing up at the cupboards that held their current mismatched dinnerware.

"We're going to get rid of this old stuff," declared Cassandra. "We'll give it to Goodwill or somebody." She started pulling their old plates out of the cupboard and carrying them to the dining room table.

"First, we'll empty out the cupboard. Next, we'll wash and dry the new dishes and put them in the cupboard. And then we'll put the old dishes in the box and hide it in the closet until Chuck can come back and help me take it somewhere." She gestured excitedly in between trips from the kitchen cupboard to the dining room table and back. "I can't wait to see Mom's face when she opens the cupboard the first time and sees all these pretty dishes!"

"Does Mom *want* new dishes?" Isabelle asked.

"Of course she does, silly!" Cassandra started running hot water into the sink, then added a healthy squirt of Joy dish soap. "She won't have to be embarrassed anymore by all those old plates and cups that don't match anything."

"Our mom was embarrassed?" Felicity wondered.

"She had to be." Cassandra was emphatic. "Wouldn't anybody?" She turned to Felicity who was standing nearest the large carton. "Can you reach the plates? Let's start with the dinner plates."

Felicity stood on her tiptoes, reached in and carefully pulled out a plate. "They *are* pretty. Mom's really going to like them."

"She'll sure be surprised," Isabelle commented.

When the new dishes had been all unpacked and washed, then carefully placed in the cupboard for Mom to discover, the girls sat at the dining room table with their homework assignments. Papers were shuffled, book pages riffled, pencils chewed.

"What time does the kitchen clock say?" Cassandra demanded of Isabelle, who was seated so she could view that clock.

"Nine-twenty."

"Shouldn't she be home by now?" Felicity asked.

"Sometimes that bus runs a little late—it's the one everyone catches when the stores are about to close." Isabelle offered a practical explanation.

"Shhh. I think I hear her coming!" Cassandra leaned over the table with her ear cocked as if in a cartoon. Sure enough, the knob on the back door turned, Cassandra buried her nose in her book in feigned study, and their mom came into the kitchen.

"Oh, hi, Mom." Cassandra's exaggerated nonchalance would have been transparent if their mom had been alert—but she wasn't, she was tired. She half-heartedly held a small white paper sack out to them.

"Hi, girls. I'm afraid there's not much here, only some regular cinnamon and sugars. We were very busy. Lots of shoppers downtown. At least some people have money to spend." She shrugged her coat off and held it in her arms as she surveyed the trio before her. "How's the homework coming?"

"Fine," Isabelle assured her mother.

"Would you like a cup of coffee?" Cassandra asked. "I could make a pot so you could have some with your donut."

"Oh, Cassandra—I'm not going to have a donut. It's the last thing I want to look at right now. And coffee would keep me awake."

"How about a cup of tea?" Even Isabelle was eager to advance the plot. "That'll help you relax."

"Oh, I was ready to go straight to bed…" She observed the disappointment on her daughters' faces. "But tea might be nice."

"I'll put the kettle on," Isabelle moved past her mother into the kitchen. While her mother went to hang up her coat, she busied herself filling the kettle with water and placing it on the burner. When she started to open the cupboard to take out a cup and saucer, Cassandra hissed at her.

"No! Let Mom open the cupboard!" She motioned for Isabelle to come back to her place at the dining room table. Isabelle stood for a moment, uncertain. Then she opened another cupboard and took out the box of Lipton teabags and set it on the counter.

"Isabelle!" Cassandra implored her sister.

"What's going on?" Mom asked as she came back to the dining room. Isabelle hurriedly took her chair.

"Nothing," Felicity said, contradicting herself with a wide, revealing grin.

"Okay, what's up?" Mom directed her question to Cassandra.

"Nothing. We're doing our homework. Want to have your tea here?" She moved some papers to clear a space in front of the one empty chair.

In the nick of time, the kettle whistled. Mom went into the kitchen and turned the burner off, then turned to open the cupboard for a cup and saucer. As she did so, all three girls rose slightly from their chairs and craned to see what her reaction would be.

"What's this?!" Mom looked at the girls in true bewilderment. "Whose dishes are these?"

"They're ours!" Felicity cried.

"They're yours, Mom," Cassandra clarified.

"But where did they come from?"

"Cassandra bought them," Isabelle explained.

"With her paychecks," Felicity added. "Aren't they beautiful?"

"Do you like them, Mom?" Cassandra asked.

Mom took a cup out of the cupboard then, and held it up to examine it closely. "Well, of course I like them. They are *beautiful*." She paused, then took a saucer to fit under the cup. She hesitated, looking from the cupboard to her daughters, then dropped a teabag in the new cup and poured boiling water over it. She brought her tea to the table and sat down next to Cassandra. She blew a little into the steaming hot liquid, then took a sip. "My tea even tastes better in this pretty cup," she declared, smiling around at her daughters, who beamed with accomplishment.

Then she reached over and gave Cassandra's arm a squeeze. "But really, sweetie, you should have spent that money on a new winter coat for yourself."

The new dishes were almost regarded as everyday dishes by the time—a few weeks later—Cassandra came home from school one late morning. Her mother was ironing at the board set up in her bedroom, her usual spot. Cassandra somehow thought she could sneak upstairs and go to bed, but her mother's bedroom was right there at the bottom of the stairs.

"Cassandra! What's wrong? Why aren't you in school?" Her mother set the iron up and hung the blouse she was ironing on a hanger.

"I don't feel so good."

Her mother unplugged the iron and went to her daughter. She put a hand to Cassandra's forehead. "Are you running a fever? Do you have a sore throat?"

"No, kind of an upset stomach." Cassandra turned to go upstairs, but her mother put her hand on her arm.

"Have you been throwing up?"

"A little," Cassandra admitted, turning back to her mother but not looking her in the eye.

Her mother studied her. "Cassandra?"

"Chuck and I are going to get married!"

"Married? When? Not now! In five years after you've graduated from college?"

"No. Soon. As soon as possible."

"Oh, Cassandra." Her mother tightened her grip on Cassandra's arm.

"Yep. I think I might be P-G." Cassandra tried a brave grin.

"Cassandra, Cassandra." Her mother pulled her oldest daughter to her in a sad hug. "I was afraid this would happen," her mother admitted. "I tried to warn you…"

She felt her daughter crumble and begin to sob.

"Mom, I'm so scared. Will it hurt? I didn't know it could happen so fast. We only did it once.."

"Well, maybe you aren't really pregnant?" her mother suggested. "Maybe you have the flu." She patted her daughter on the back and brought her into her bedroom so they could sit side by side on the bed.

"I've missed my period. I'm three weeks late." Cassandra fingered the tufts of the rose-colored chenille spread.

"Oh." Cassandra's mom paused, considering. "Well, that's a pretty good indication. You probably *are* pregnant."

She took her daughter's hand. "Does Chuck know?" Cassandra nodded. "What does he think?"

"He was pretty surprised." Cassandra looked up at her mother. "But he wants to get married. He says he always wanted kids." Her chin jutted out a bit. "And besides, he loves me."

"Love? It's going to take more than love—whatever you think that is. You're so young, Cassandra!"

"I'll be seventeen by the time the baby is born. Lots of people have babies when they're seventeen. Younger, even."

"So this is February..." Her mother counted off the months on her fingers. "March, April, May, ..."

"October. The baby will be due in October." Cassandra has figured this out.

"You could at least finish out this school year."

"Mom, I'll be showing by then and I'm not going to go to school in maternity clothes!" The defiant daughter returned, stood and confronted her mother. "Besides, I'm going to get married and work more hours at Grant's until the baby comes... so I can save up money for baby stuff..."

"But where will you live?"

"Chuck's uncle owns an apartment building over on Royal Avenue. He says he can get us our own little apartment. Chuck was going to move out of his parents' house soon anyway." She took a breath. "It'll just be a little sooner."

"Well, that's lucky! It sounds as if you and Chuck have worked things out." She stood and hugged her young daughter's rigid frame. "I want you to be sure this is what you want. There *are* other options. What if—in a few years—you regret not having gone to college, not becoming a teacher?"

"I can always go back to school later if I want." Cassandra has made up her mind. There are no traces of her earlier tears.

"I guess…" Her mother sank back down on the bed, not nearly as certain as this headstrong daughter.

"But it's a good thing Chuck hasn't hauled away those old dishes yet. I mean, could we have them? We were going to give them to Goodwill."

"Of course. And I have a couple of books of S & H Green Stamps—you could use those to get a fry-pan, or something." Her mother reached out to take Cassandra's hand. "And that morning sickness should go away in a couple of months, so you'll be feeling better."

"Actually, I feel better already. I'll probably go back to school for sixth and seventh hour."

Her mother shook her head in bewilderment. What sense did it make to go back for an afternoon when Cassandra would be leaving school permanently in a matter of weeks?

"We're reading 'Catcher in the Rye' in English and I love that book!"

Did she know it'd be a long time before she'd read a book again? Cassandra's mother rose and turned quickly back to the ironing board, plugged in the iron. Swallowed the tears rising in her throat.

"You might try a couple of soda crackers," she advised.

A month later, after Chuck and Cassandra had "eloped" to City Hall for a quick unceremonious tying of the knot, they were settling into their tiny apartment.

Chuck hauled the box of dishes into the kitchen as Cassandra finished lining the final cupboard with shelf paper.

"I know these are clean so I can put them right in the cupboard," Cassandra explained to Chuck as she opened the box and reached in.

She unwrapped tissue from the first piece and emitted a small gasp.

"Look, Chuck." She held the pretty white cup with the pale pink rose out for her new husband to see. "Mom gave us the good dishes."

Bridal Registry

As Rosalie exited the elevator on the third floor at the Belmont, she saw her father deep in a chess game with one of his friends.

"Hi, Pop," she said, bending down to brush his cheek with a kiss, then addressed his opponent. "How are you, Mr. Collura?"

"How does it look? Your father has no empathy for an old man." He made a feeble gesture at the chessboard and then shoved his wheelchair back from the table. "I'm glad you're here, Rosalie. You're rescuing me from another embarrassing defeat at the hands of this tyrant."

"He's always been that way, Mr. Collura. A heartless competitor."

Her father grinned at her. "What's the point, if it's not to win?"

"I'll leave you two," Jasper Collura said, wheeling away from the table.

"He looks tired," Rosalie said.

"Yeah, he's not doing so well," her dad agreed. "I probably should have let him win."

Rosalie smiled. "Do you want to go to your room?"

"No, I like it out here where I can keep track of everybody." He moved back from the table a little in his own wheelchair and glanced around the living room-like area. Rosalie sat down in one of the comfortable armchairs next to him.

There were three tables: the one in the middle of the room had a puzzle on it that was halfway to completion, the table on the far side was occupied by four women amiably making their way through a card game, and then there was this table—designated for a game of checkers or chess. The chairs were upholstered with a soft rose-colored fabric and had sturdy arms to make it easier to get in and out of them. Nearby, a tall, impossibly thin man sat on a sofa reading the sports section from this morning's *Tribune*. Three dark green sofas were arranged in separate groupings with additional armchairs. The end tables had side racks on them to hold newspapers and magazines.

Rosalie had decided, after just a few visits, that it was the lighting that made this area so hospitable. Rather than the harsh overhead fluorescent fixtures they had encountered in the other retirement facilities they had visited, here were nondescript table lamps and floor lamps—similar to what most of the residents must have had in their own homes.

Her father was watching her survey their surroundings. "It's nice here," he said, leaning over to pat her on the arm. "I like it."

"I know, Pop. You keep telling me that. But what I said still stands—if this doesn't work out, you are still more than welcome to move in with me."

"Don't even talk about it. I'm happy here; and I like knowing I'm not cramping the style of my gorgeous Rosalie."

Her father still thought Rosalie, nearing fifty, might have suitors coming to call. Did she? Would she end up at The Belmont with no one coming to visit her on Sunday afternoons?

Rosalie smiled approvingly at Marika Casey when she showed up for her appointment on Tuesday. This time she was with her fiancé, Paul Hitchens, instead of with her mother, who had brought Marika in unannounced last week. At the time, they had made an official bridal registry appointment for this afternoon, and Rosalie had delicately suggested that Marika's husband-to-be would more likely be eating off the dishes and more frequently assisting in the kitchen than would Marika's mother. "Well, he's not much of a cook, but he does like to eat," Marika had responded, laughing and actually turning a little pink. The blushing bride.

Marika Casey was not a child; Rosalie pegged her at thirty-three, thirty-four—her fiancé seemed to Rosalie to be a few years younger. Both Marika and Paul had the kinds of jobs where they could get away on a weekday afternoon to meet with Rosalie for the couple of hours or more it would take them to go through the china, linens, housewares, bed and bath departments. And, as was the case with so many couples, they were living together but were mostly making-do with a combined collection of hand-me-downs.

"When I got my first apartment," Paul said, "My mom gave me what was left of our everyday dishes and went out and got herself a whole new set. For *twelve* people."

"Your mom's no dummy," Marika observed.

Rosalie nodded and asked Paul, "Do you like your dishes?"

"Mine? The hand-me-downs? They're okay."

"There's like five plates left," Marika said.

"I've moved a couple of times—what do you want from me?"

"Well, let's choose some things you'll really like so you'll be taking very good care of them," Rosalie suggested, picking up a clipboard and walking toward the display of good china.

"This stuff looks very breakable," Paul said.

"It is, that's why you'll have to take good care of it," Rosalie said, smiling at Paul, who immediately turned and grinned at Marika.

"That'll be Marika's department. You don't want me anywhere near this stuff," he said.

Rosalie paused a moment, half-expecting some sort of good-natured retort from Marika, but she just grinned back at Paul. "He's right—Paul's the proverbial bull in a china shop. In fact, let's establish right now that Paul can look at, but does not touch, anything in this department."

Now it was Paul's turn to blush—but he didn't seem actually embarrassed—more like pleased with having been tagged with this stereotypical male flaw. He seemed to puff up a little, flexed his biceps under his suit coat. Just because he was an accountant didn't mean he wasn't a jock. Definitely not a wimp.

Rosalie looked from Paul to Marika, who was also beaming, and smiled back at them. "Let's start over here in the Wedgwood department. I'll show you a couple of our more popular patterns and you can tell me what you like or don't like about them and we'll go from there."

They both nodded and followed along obediently. Rosalie picked up a sparkling white dinner plate embellished with a white lace motif. "This is Wedgwood's 'English Lace,' a favorite of couples who want something traditional for their good china."

Marika took the plate from Rosalie and studied it. "Maybe we're not all that traditional," Marika said, handing it back.

"But Wedgwood's good stuff, right?" countered Paul.

Rosalie could feel this was going to be a long afternoon. They moved on to the more contemporary patterns.

She was tired as she headed home from work that night. It hadn't been an extraordinarily busy day—although the registry of Marika and Paul had seemed to take forever. The couple didn't have very similar tastes; Marika had been immediately drawn to the very contemporary Kate Spade "Gardner Street" with its lovely green foliage, while Paul seemed to prefer the more traditional Waterford "Ballet Icing"—although Rosalie suspected he was simply impressed with the name "Waterford," and had likely never heard of Kate Spade.

Just choosing their fine china had taken a half-hour and Rosalie had finally figured out she needed to show Paul merchandise manufactured by names he recognized. That made things progress a little more efficiently, but soon Rosalie grew tired of Paul. Everything was an investment. What did Marika see in him, she wondered?

Some matches were obvious, some were unfathomable.

Marika marrying Paul seemed *almost* as inconceivable as Rosalie taking up with her building's new custodian—Matthew, she thought his name was. Nice enough fellow, and good-looking in a low key kind of way, but obviously not dating material for Rosalie. She first laid eyes on him when he came up to fix her toilet a few weeks ago. The building's previous custodian, Tony, had retired after many years of attempting to fix that toilet—it either didn't completely flush, or would run on and on for a long time after flushing. Come to think of it, she hadn't had any problems with it since that Matthew had worked on it. But it had only been a few weeks.

The last time Rosalie had anything like a date was almost a year ago when one of her Book Babes had fixed her up with a cousin who was newly divorced and in town for a visit. "You'll love him, Rosalie," Sarah had enthused. "He's very good-looking, in terrific shape, and he has a nice little dental practice back in Boise. And the divorce wasn't his fault—his wife was some kind of prima donna."

The date with Wayne was going pretty well—dinner at one of Rosalie's favorite places, Mon Ami Gabi. He had lived in Chicago before moving to Idaho, so they had that in common. The conversation moved along as they discussed the Bulls and the Bears—although he was now a Seattle Seahawks fan. Moving on to other subjects, Rosalie asked him what he'd been reading.

"I don't really have a lot of time for reading," Wayne said. "I work out a lot when I'm not in the office and the rest of the time just seems to evaporate into thin air."

"Have you ever tried to read while you work out?" Rosalie asked.

"Naw, I just watch the TVs they have all over the gym. Catch up on the Seahawks that way...and the rest of the news," he added.

"Well, that's convenient," Rosalie said. Afterward, she realized he was probably as bored with her as she had been with him. She hadn't even known who the Seahawks' quarterback was.

Now, Rosalie collected her mail in her apartment building's foyer, then pushed the elevator button. When the door opened, Rosalie was surprised to see Matt—not in his usual work clothes, but in a blue-and-white-checked shirt and khakis, with a lightbulb in one hand and a couple of books in the other.

"Going up?" he asked, holding the door open as Rosalie hesitated.

"Uh, yes, I am. I thought maybe you were getting off." Rosalie stepped inside and Matt leaned over to press SEVEN, the number for her floor, then DOOR CLOSE.

"Nope, gotta deliver this three-way to Mrs. Fitzgerald on ELEVEN before I can head out." Matt gestured at her with the coiled white bulb.

She nodded. Rosalie was curious to see what sort of books her building's custodian was carrying, but she didn't want to appear nosy…or interested. Silence filled the elevator's small space, interspersed with the little ding as the elevator passed each floor, carrying them upward. They were on the fourth floor already.

"You okay on bulbs?" Matt asked.

"I am…yes. Thanks."

Ding.

Silence.

Ding.

Abruptly, Rosalie nodded toward the books in Matt's hand—"Are you a reader then?"

"Yup. Haven't quite graduated to the e-books." He held up the couple of volumes, slick in their plastic covers, his large hand obscuring the titles. "I found that branch library over on Fullerton, makes it real handy."

She had to know. "What are you reading?"

"I just got around to reading this Verghese book—figured I'd better get to it before they make a movie out of it and there's a long wait list."

"Did you like it?" The words were out so quickly, she almost put a hand to her mouth.

Ding. The door opened for her floor.

"I really did. Lots of medical jargon toward the end, but the story sure is a good one." Matt used his lightbulb hand to hold the door open. "How about you? Have you read it?"

She nodded. "My mother was Catholic and the revelation about the nun sort of blew my mind."

"And all that stuff about growing up in Ethiopia," Matt said. "That was kinda cool."

"Have you ever been to Africa?" Even as she asked, Rosalie thought the question sort of preposterous. She stopped in the door opening, waiting for his answer.

The elevator door jerked at Matt's hand. "Actually, I was there for a stint in the Peace Corps," he said, moving to hold the DOOR OPEN button, as Rosalie stepped into the hall.

"Really? Then…have you read '*A Long Way Gone*?'"

Matt released the DOOR OPEN button and stepped out into the hall. "The Ishmael Beah book? Yeah, that's one of the best things I've read in the last few years. He was here within the last year for the Printer's Row festival, or the Humanities thing, can't remember which."

Rosalie stood gawking at this custodian in a regular man's clothing, carrying real books. She realized he was aware of the impression he was making as he carefully returned her stare. She looked away from his steady gaze, back to the books in his hand.

"How's the toilet working?" Matt gestured again with the lightbulb, toward her apartment door a few steps away.

"Oh, fine!" She smiled and took a couple of steps in that direction. He pushed the elevator button.

"Well, you don't need to have something broke to call me." She gave him a quizzical look.

"Like to borrow a book or…a cup of sugar," he explained, and then the elevator opened and took him away.

Inside her apartment, Rosalie tied on an apron over her work clothes. Rosalie knew her father looked forward to the Tuesday night dinners at her apartment, and she did, too. It was a bit of a hassle getting her father from The Belmont to her apartment and back again, but the nursing home used a van service to transport folks in wheelchairs and it was worth it to give him a change of scenery. Besides, she liked cooking for someone other than just herself; she took pride in her ability to prepare a nice meal and set a pretty table.

Tonight they were having one of her father's favorites—
Chicken Parmesan. Rosalie had actually browned the chicken
breasts the night before and covered them with tomato sauce
before she put them in the fridge. When she got home from
work, she just sprinkled the tops with freshly-grated parmesan
and slid the yellow Crueset casserole dish in the oven; the
apartment was already beginning to fill with the fabulous scent
of tomatoes and garlic and roasted red peppers.

She had set the table last night, too—using her mother's
delicate good china with the narrow border of blue flowers—
dishes that had automatically gone to Rosalie as the only child.
Often when she cooked Italian, Rosalie liked to use her brightly
colored dinnerware from Florence, actually purchased here at
her Chicago department store. For tonight's dinner with Pop,
though, Rosalie had carefully arranged the dinner plates and
silverware that had been used for many special family occasions.
She pictured her parents beaming happily over a table crowded
with aunts, uncles and cousins—her mother had a large extended family that gathered every Sunday at her parents' home
and helped make up for the fact that Rosalie had no siblings.

Now, as she folded the crisply ironed blue cloth napkins
and centered them on the plates, she realized her thoughts had
strayed to that custodian guy—Matt. She found herself wondering what kind of family he came from; was he even from
Chicago? Why had she been surprised to learn that he was an
avid reader—did she think all custodians were illiterate?

Rosalie was startled by the ringing of the doorbell; she
had been half-waiting for the intercom to buzz notifying her
that her father was being dropped off downstairs so she could
go down and greet him. She hurried to the door and peered
through the peep-hole. It was her dad, all right. She opened
the door to find her dad, with a smiling Matt behind him.

"Pop! You didn't call from downstairs?"

"Didn't have to. This nice fella said he was going up, he'd give me a push."

Rosalie looked at Matt questioningly.

"I was just coming back from the library and here was this important-looking gentleman in the vestibule who claimed to be your father. Wanted to be sure everything was on the up and up," Matt said.

"Well, thank you. Yes, I wouldn't say he's exactly harmless, but Pop probably doesn't represent any serious threat." She gave her father's wheelchair a little tug to help him get over the threshold and then he wheeled right on past her.

"Boy! Sure smells good in here!" her father exclaimed.

Matt stood smiling in the still open door.

"Would you like to come in?" Rosalie asked.

"No, thanks, I can't. But your dad's right—it smells terrific. You must be a good cook."

Her father whirled his chair around. "She is—Rosalie's every bit as good a cook as her mother was. Smells like Chicken Parmesan, Rosy—is it?"

She nodded. Then felt obliged to say to Matt: "Are you sure you won't join us?"

"No, really. I can't. But…I'll take a raincheck."

"Every Tuesday night," her father chimed in. "She cooks like this for me every Tuesday night. Wanna come next week?"

Matt laughed. He looked at Rosalie and winked. "Well, we'll see how the cook is feeling next week." He took hold of the doorknob to pull it closed. "You two have a pleasant evening." Rosalie stood with her hand on the door for a moment, holding it open. "Seriously, I'll take a raincheck," Matt said. "Call me if you need anything." The door was closed, and he was gone.

"Seems like a nice fella," her father said.

"Come into the kitchen while I make the salad," Rosalie said. "You can pour us a glass of wine."

"Don't you think he's a nice fella?" her father persisted, wheeling after her and up to the kitchen table where she had an open bottle of Sangiovese and a pair of wine glasses.

"Pop, I just met the guy. I mean, he just started here as custodian a few weeks ago. I don't really know him."

"But wasn't it nice the way he brought me up here?"

"Of course it was," Rosalie had to smile at her father. "Wait a minute, are you two in cahoots or something?"

"Not yet, but I can't make any promises." He grinned and poured the wine. "Neither one of us is getting any younger, you know."

Rosalie threw a pot holder at her father.

Later, as they sat lingering over a couple of cannolis and coffee, Rosalie's father waggled his finger at her. "Now, you know I was teasing before, but seriously, Rosy—you should invite a nice guy like that Matt person to dinner. What could it hurt?"

"I know, Pop. But don't worry about me so much. I like my life the way it is."

"Of course you do—but I think you'd discover you'd like it even more if you had someone to cuddle up with at night."

"Pop!"

"And it's not just sex you're missing out on. It's sharing a nice dinner like this—I'm not gonna be around forever. You'll have to find another date one of these days. I want you to have the companionship your mother and I had for so many good years."

"You and Mom did have a good marriage, didn't you? You always seemed to be having such a good time."

"Whoa! Wait a minute." Her father set his coffee cup down in its saucer with a clang. "It wasn't *always* hunky-dory. We had our moments."

"But they were 'moments.' I worry about making a mistake and choosing somebody I'll end up quibbling with over every little thing forever. 'Til death do us part' is a long time, even if you're 'older' when you take the plunge." She paused with her fork in the air, a chunk of cannoli balanced on the end. "It must have been because you and Mom had so much in common that your marriage worked out so well."

Her father chuckled. "Now, Rosy. Think about it. Your mother and I really did not have that much in common. She was raised Catholic, and while my family wasn't strict about it—I was raised in the Jewish faith. Your mother came from a huge well-to-do family—relatives all over the north side of Chicago. I was the only child of a schoolteacher—transplanted from an itty-bitty town in Ohio. And, don't forget, your mother was eight years older than me. We didn't even like the same music because she was pre-rock-and-roll!"

"Then how did you make it work?"

"For one thing, neither us had any desire to 'quibble about every little thing'." She was amused to see her father use air quotes. "Some people live to quarrel, we didn't. You don't. You'd figure out quick enough if someone gets his undies in a bundle over every little thing."

"I don't know, Pop."

"Of course you don't. I read a poem the other day about marriage being like a bungee jump. There aren't any guarantees." He looked at her and put down his coffee cup, gently this time. He clasped his hands in his lap and leaned forward, almost nose to nose with his daughter.

"But, Rosy—nothing ventured, nothing gained. Sometimes you gotta take a chance."

"I know, Pop. I know." She stood and gave her father a hug, then began to clear the dishes.

Later, when Rosalie took her father downstairs for his transport back to The Belmont, she dawdled in the vestibule, checking her mailbox again although she knew she had taken what mail there was upstairs earlier. And when she got on the elevator, she held the door open a minute, waiting to see if someone would come along to share the ride. It was very quiet.

As she ran water into the sink, bubbles billowing over the couple of wine glasses, she glanced over at the wall phone and saw the little card stuck behind it. She dried her hands on the dishtowel and walked over to the phone, picked up the receiver, and dialed.

"Hello?" he said, after just one ring.

Home Plate

Fenton is on third, the incredible hulk poised to come barreling into me at home plate if Calivari gets any kind of a hit. It's 120 degrees on the field and I'm melting in all this catcher's gear. The count goes to 3-2 on Calivari, and I give Glazer, our gazillion-dollar closer, the sign for a high fast ball, out of the zone. I figure Calivari will whiff it and we can all go home. But, no, Glazer misses his mark and Calivari dinks it into right center and the throw comes to me at the same time that fucker Fenton is slamming into me.

While everybody else goes home I'm getting pictures taken of my left leg which crunched menacingly under Fenton when we collided. I'm a hero because I hung onto the ball and Fenton was out, but I'm also on the DL for who knows how long and then I'll probably get sent to Des Moines for rehab. I spent too many weeks in Iowa last year, most of the summer—for chrissakes. *This* summer I've been living in a furnished condo in a great high-rise a block off Michigan Avenue. It's the same building Mike Ditka lives in, accommodations I deserve after putting in so many years in the minors—but now I have to go back to some desolate digs along the lovely Raccoon River in the middle of Iowa cornfields.

I'm too old for this crap. Thirty-seven is old in baseball years—a fact of which I've been made painfully aware. But everything finally fell into place this year—the Cubs brought in Glazer for a bucketload of cash and knew that I had caught him off and on in Knoxville with good results. So they brought me up to the Big Show and I connected. Glazer cooperated, let me call most of the pitches, and we were regarded as a sure win when it was our turn. Also, for some reason, I was getting a few hits. Even on the days I wasn't the starting catcher, Muldoon would put me in to pinch-hit late in the game. At long last, I was where I belonged.

And now I wasn't. Back to Des Moines. I still had stuff there in a storage unit because frankly, back in April, I wasn't sure if I'd be Big Time for two weeks or two months or two years.

"You could always hang it up and go in the car business with me," Mickey said when he called. My brother read the bad news in the Sports section of the Iowa City Press-Citizen. He has a dealership in Coralville and is doing well for himself.

"I don't think I'd be good at that," I told him. Which begged the question—what would I be good at? I'd worked as a line cook at the Beefstro during the off-season, but I didn't relish going back to a minimum wage existence. Fortunately, I hadn't gone all crazy when I was called up—except for the cool digs—so I'd been stashing most of the big bucks and now I was in pretty good shape financially. When Alicia and I got divorced I was still playing Single A ball, so there was no alimony involved. As a paralegal, she was making more than I was back in those days.

"You should go back to school," Alicia advised. We still talked now and then. She called, all sympathetic but without fully disguising the I-told-you-so tone in her voice. Alicia had gone to school while she worked and passed the bar without breaking a sweat. She was "of counsel" for one of Des Moines' many insurance companies.

"Probably not," I said. The only reason I went to college was because I got a baseball scholarship. And I couldn't imagine being on a campus with a bunch of twenty-year-olds. Even the girls scare me. Especially the girls.

I'm in the training room doing some of the fun exercises the PT guy has dreamed up to further punish me when Scott from Public Relations sticks his head in the door. "There's a reporter here from the public radio station wants to talk to you. Okay if I send her in?"

Public radio? Her? Those two red flags don't dissuade me. What the hell. "Sure. Why not?"

I continue to sweat and grunt in my most impressive manner as this reporter person makes her entrance. Right away I see why she's in radio and not TV. This is a big woman. Not fat, really—I guess you'd call her chunky. And tall. I mean, I'm not quite six feet tall, right? And this woman is right up there— she could be taller than me. She's got something purple going on in her otherwise dark hair, dangly earrings with feathers in 'em, and a short skirt revealing killer legs in high heels.

She walks right up and sticks out her hand. "Hi. I'm Stella Stephens from WBEZ. Thanks for agreeing to talk with me."

"Sure. No problem," I say, huffing and puffing to full effect.

"Um, is there a better time to do this? How much longer will you be working out? I hate to interrupt."

"Oh." She wants more than a few words. "That's okay. I'm just about done." I perform another maneuver enabling me to steal a glance at those legs again, then sit up and fling my own legs over the exercise table. "You know where the Salt & Pepper is down on Clark? Why don't I meet you there in fifteen minutes?"

"That'd be great. I really appreciate it. See you in a bit." She turns and sashays out on those high heels. I head to the showers.

I hobble over to the Salt & Pepper on crutches and slide into the booth Stella the Reporter has snagged. We both order burgers and fries, and she tells me she is doing a story about the precariousness of being a big league ballplayer. "One minute you're barely making minimum wage," she explains, "and the next you're pulling down really big bucks."

"And back again." I nod in rhythm to vigorously salting my fries and hand the shaker to her. "Tell me about it."

"I want *you* to tell *me* about it." The woman also likes a lot of salt on her fries.

"Oh, right."

"Like—how long were you in the minor leagues before you made it to the majors? Do you mind if I ask your age?"

She can look up my age on the team roster, probably already has. I attempt to collect my thoughts. She continues.

"I mean, what was that like? Can you compare the two experiences?"

"I'm thirty-seven." She nods. I was right, she has looked it up. "This is my first full season in the majors. I've been called up before, mostly in September when they can expand their roster, but sometimes for a week or two when a regular catcher gets injured."

"You've really paid your dues."

"Yeah, it's not easy to support yourself while you're chasing the dream. Unless you've got a rich daddy or a movie star wife, you have to work other jobs in the off season while you keep yourself in shape for the next Opening Day."

"You don't have either one of those?" she asks.

"What?"

"Rich daddy or movie star wife?"

"My dad passed a couple of years ago—I would have loved to have him around this summer to see me playing regular at Wrigley."

"Sorry."

"And the only wife I ever had divorced me years ago."

"In some ways, it must be easier on your own." She says it as an observation but it's a question.

"It is, but you get tired of that, too. Being alone." I stop. This isn't what I want to tell a reporter. She's hanging on every word. Her little tape recorder going. "Can you turn that thing off for a bit?"

"Um, sure." She hits a button. "Is the interview over?"

"It's just that—somehow it got kind of personal."

"Sorry."

"No, it's not your fault. I think people should know about the disparity there is between trying to eke out an existence in the minor leagues and making it to the Bigs."

"That's what I thought," she says, swishing a fry around in the scattering of salt at the edge of her plate.

"It must be kind of like working for public radio instead of having some big network job." My turn to make an observation.

"I *like* public radio." She points a fry at me.

Uh-oh, I've struck a nerve. "Me too. Morning Edition. Wait, Wait, Don't Tell Me."

"But you're right. I'm not making the big bucks."

"So do you have a rich daddy or a movie star husband?" Seems a fair question.

"No, but I have a married sister with a spare bedroom in Jefferson Park."

"Ah-ha."

"Not exactly the circumstances I'd hoped I'd find myself in in my mid-thirties, but I'm doing okay. I like my work. I get to meet some interesting people...." She lets that hang out there and looks me in the eye.

I'm in. "Tell you what. Let me pull together some of my payroll figures so you'll have an accurate accounting of the actual difference. Are you on some sort of time constraint? We could get together again for dinner. How late do you work?"

Now she back-pedals. "I can't tonight, I've got to cover a City Council meeting." Pause. "But how about tomorrow night?"

"Tomorrow night's good. I'm *not* working," I point out, giving her my most rueful smile and nodding toward my crutches leaning against the wall.

"Oh, right." She grants me a little chuckle and pulls a business card out of her jacket pocket. "Here's how you can reach me. Call and let me know when and where to meet you. If I don't answer, just leave a message."

I reach for the check as I struggle to my feet. "Still making the big bucks at the moment."

"No, seriously," she protests. "I'll expense this." When she stands I realize this chick actually *is* taller than me. Whoa.

"C'mon," I object. She's got the check and is headed to the counter.

"You can get dinner tomorrow night," she says, over her shoulder. Does that make it a date instead of business?

"It's a deal."

There's no game the next day so all I have is a couple hours in the training room. First thing in the morning I text Stella. "*Dinner's at my place, 171 East Chicago, Apt. 53A. 6:30.*" I wait a couple hours for her to text back that I'm out of my gourd, but she doesn't, so after I get back from the workout I hobble over to Trader Joe's. I have to take a taxi back—have you ever tried managing crutches and a couple sacks of groceries?

I put the Sinskey rosé in the fridge to chill and spend the rest of the afternoon chopping and slicing and marinating. We're going to have my Killer Breast of Duck with a nice little couscous and some roasted vegetables. I set the table using Aunt Miriam's good dishes that she passed on to me when she moved into the old folks' home. Good thing they weren't in storage in the middle of Iowa. Even when I cook just for myself, I like to use nice plates and silverware. I've got a thing for presentation. I like to pretend I'm a big-time chef in a classy restaurant.

At 6:35, the doorman phones that there's a "Miss Stephens" on the way up. I pull the wine out of the fridge, uncork it and light the candles—the whole schmear. The doorbell rings and when I open the door, there's Stella Stephens but now she's a couple inches shorter. She's wearing one of those white lacey off-the-shoulder summer tops and black pants and flats and some kind of perfume that smells like vanilla. She hands me a 6-pack of Stella.

"I wasn't sure what we were having, so I just brought beer. I figured if we didn't drink it tonight, it wouldn't go to waste."

"You shouldn't have," I say, glancing at her feet.

She smiles and then is distracted by the view. "Ohmigod! Look at this. Wow, you can see all the way up Lake Shore Drive."

"Yeah, I'm lucky this corner unit was open." I take her elbow and guide her over to the dining area. "You can see Navy Pier out this side."

"Wow" again. She gapes a minute, then turns—"Will you have to give this up? I mean, if you're going back to Des Moines?"

"Probably. But it's mine for the moment and I'm going to enjoy it."

She takes a few steps toward the kitchen area. "It smells fabulous in here. I guess we're not having pizza?"

"No, no pizza tonight. Sorry. How about a glass of wine?" She follows me into the kitchen where I put the Stella six-pack in the fridge, then pour a glass of rosé for each of us. "Let's go back into the living room."

She stops to read the only thing I've hung on the wall since I moved in. It's a framed copy of one of my favorite quotes:

> *In a hard game played by hard men, catchers are the hardest of men. They take a physical beating every night; they are the guys with the mangled fingers, scarred knees and dented foreheads. They are the most involved players in every game; they are the brains and the brawn of the operation at the same time. They are the only guys who wear full armor; they are the only players on the field who face the other way.* **Tim Kurkjian, ESPN Magazine.**

"The 'brains and the brawn,' hmmm?" She gives me a look.

"I try. Sometimes I'm not brainy enough to get out of the way of the brawn." I limp my way over to the couch where I've set out a plate of olives and cheese.

Stella remains standing after I've sat down. She does a careful 360° of the place. "So does a maid service come with these digs?"

"Nah. They have one if you want, but I'm kinda fussy so there's no sense in me paying someone to come in and do something I'd just do all over again."

"You cook ...and you clean?"

I'm not sure how to take the look of disbelief on her face. "Guilty as charged." I pat the couch next to me. "Sit, why don't you?"

"How can you still be single?" A thought crosses her face. "You are single, aren't you?"

"Guilty again." She sits as I attempt to explain my current lack of a spouse. "I guess I've been a little pre-occupied with trying to make it to the Bigs. And now that I'm here, I find I have to be careful about fending off the starstruck or the gold-diggers."

"Awww. I feel sorry for you." She puts her hand on my knee momentarily, a fleeting gesture of faux sympathy. I quell the stirrings this arouses in me—there is dinner, after all.

Dinner went well. The sun was going down over the Chicago skyline as we had dessert—slices of plum tart I had purchased because I thought they'd go well with the duck and didn't have time to make myself. The lights of the Ferris wheel on Navy Pier blinked behind us.

"Do I smell coffee?" she asks, stirring from sleep the next morning.

"You do. But it'll keep." I like kissing this woman all over her big voluptuous body.

"You take very good care of home plate," she observes.

"I try."

We sit at the kitchen table with coffee and toasted poppy-seed bagels. "Why do you have purple hair?" I ask.

"Does it bother you?"

"I'm just curious." I want to know what makes this woman tick.

"I can't stay," she says, picking up stray seeds from her plate with her tongue-moistened forefinger. "I have to be at the station by nine." She stands and picks up her plate and coffee cup to take them to the kitchen. She's wearing only the lacey top from the night before; it comes to just below her butt. "If I could use your shower, I won't have to go home and I can make it to work on time."

So she showers and is gone.

I stuck my foot in my mouth with the question about her purple hair and now I'm going to be stuck in Iowa without my fancy apartment and without *Stella*. I picture Marlon Brando yelling over and over again as I drive my packed Subaru along I-80 West. The corn is turning brown; it's September after all. I know I won't be back at Wrigley yet this season. It's going to be a long cold winter.

I call. I text. But no Stella. Maybe she isn't interested in a minor league player.

It's funny, after just that one night, whenever I contemplate my future I kind of picture Stella being a part of it. But it's apparent that's not gonna happen and I figure I have to move on with my life. I start looking at vacant properties in Des Moines. Maybe I'll open a restaurant.

And then, one day in November, I get a text from her that says, "*Meet me at the Drake Diner at 6.*"

I'm early. I'm on a stool at the counter by 5:30, nursing a beer. I hardly recognize her when Stella walks in the door, but she comes right over to me so I know it's her. I stand, hesitate, and then hug her, hard.

"You look all different," I say, standing back to assess.

"You like?" She seems sure I will. Her dark hair is cut short, with nary a trace of purple or any other color. And she's lost weight. I can tell, even though she is wearing a nondescript beige pantsuit.

"I do—but I liked the way you looked before, too."

"I'm working on 'classy'," she explains.

"Oh, Stella. Don't ever do this again."

"Don't try to be classy?"

"Don't leave me high and dry. Lonely and longing for my gorgeous purple-haired Stella. Desperate for a word from you."

"Desperate? Really?" She laughs.

"You're a mean woman, Stella Stephens." I am too overjoyed to be angry. "I think you owe me a dinner."

Over burgers and fries—"the first fries I've had in months," Stella confesses—I attempt to clear up our major miscommunication.

"When I asked about your purple hair, it was just curiosity. I didn't mean that I didn't like your hair…or anything else about you. Think about it—would I have been so immediately attracted to you if there was something I didn't like?

"But when I saw your apartment and you served me that fancy dinner, I was pretty sure you'd be having second thoughts."

"Oh, I've had second thoughts; and third and fourth thoughts—a million thoughts about you. And you hundreds of miles away in the Big City with no interest in a bush league ballplayer."

"Well, I think it should be pretty obvious, I'm interested." She leans over and plants a salty kiss smack on the lips, right in front of whoever else was there.

"Let's get out of here," I urge, throwing some cash on the table and grabbing her arm.

She's laughing as I tug her out the diner door, headed for my two-room apartment and some careful tending of home plate.

Yard Work

I'm a fella who likes a nice lawn. I spend a lot of time mowing and clipping and bagging and blowing; fertilizing and watering and transplanting. It's kept me out of trouble in my retirement years. After I finish whatever yard work I've assigned myself for the day, I like to sit on the little wrought iron settee we have out in front of the house, pop open a Miller Lite and admire my handiwork.

It's also a good vantage point from which to keep an eye on the neighborhood. You'd be surprised at what goes on in this seemingly tranquil subdivision. The wife and I have a house smack in the middle of a cul-de-sac on a slight rise which enables me to monitor most of the houses on a couple of streets without even getting up off my settee.

I've had to call the cops a time or two when the house on the corner across the street had lots of unusual activity—cars coming and going at all hours of the day and night. Turned out my suspicions were confirmed. A nice little drug business was being conducted over there and soon enough the people who lived there were foreclosed on and had to move out. Good riddance.

The lady who moved in appears to be a single mom. There are a couple of young kids, but no man of the house that I have noticed. The lady of the house does her own yard work, and while she doesn't devote nearly the time and energy to it that I do, she does alright. And she's easy on the eyes, quite the dish. I'm guessing she's trying to get a tan while she mows the lawn and that's why she wears a kinda skimpy swimsuit—a bikini, really. She must be a nurse or something because she doesn't work Monday thru Friday; Tuesday and Wednesday are her days off and she usually mows her lawn on Tuesday afternoon, unless it rains. Then it's Wednesday. Her lawn mowing usually coincides with my settee-sitting time. And, up til now, Tuesday afternoon has been when my wife was off playing bridge.

But last week when it appeared that our new neighbor lady's lawnmower had broken down, I went over to see if I could help. I'm pretty good at fixing things.

Brenda—that's her name—was very appreciative. Turned out she hadn't been mixing the proper ratio of oil to gas, so it was a simple thing to correct and I was soon back on my settee. As a gesture of gratitude, after she finished mowing her lawn, she came across the street with a couple of cold ones—Stellas, mind you. "Thank you so much for helping me out. Mind if I join you?" So there we were, getting acquainted all neighborly like—her in her bikini and me in my Bears cap, when the wife pulled in the driveway right alongside the settee.

Next thing I know, my wife signs us up for a Civil War class that meets on Tuesday afternoons over at the Center for Learning in Retirement.

Busted.

An Old Friend

Margo was clearly agitated—but then she usually got that way when we were having company. And this was unplanned company; an old friend from high school called just this morning and said he was in town on business, was there any chance Margo and her husband would be free for dinner? Apparently he suggested we all meet at the restaurant next to his hotel, but of course Margo insisted that he come over for a "home-cooked meal," and now she was in a dither.

"Maybe we should have just met him—what's his name?"

"Don. Don Dempsey." Margo pushed around me with a handful of silverware, setting the table in rapid-fire motion.

"Maybe we should have just met this Don guy at The Olive Garden."

"The Olive Garden? Are you kidding? When we can give him a nice home-cooked meal?"

"Well, it just puts so much pressure on you at the last minute and all. Doesn't he get 'home-cooked meals' at his own house?"

"I think he's divorced." She folded napkins in some fancy way and centered them on the plates.

"Divorced?"

Margo reached around me to put the last napkin in its place. "George, you're not making it any easier. Either make yourself useful or get out of the way."

"You want me to finish setting the table?"

"I'm done—except for the water and wine glasses. You could do those. Please." Margo turned to leave the dining room and head back into the kitchen.

"Okay," I said in my most obliging manner. "The table looks nice...I see we're using the good dishes."

"What's that supposed to mean?" She stopped in the doorway to face me.

"Nothing."

"I like to use my good china when the opportunity presents itself."

"Like I say...the table looks nice. It just means you'll have to wash and dry them by hand. They can't go in the dishwasher, right?" I'm not sure why I was making an issue out of this; I knew better. I attempted to camouflage my contrariness by not looking at her, busying myself with arranging the wine glasses just so.

"George?"

I had to look up then.

"If you want to use some other dishes, feel free to set the table all over again. Otherwise, cool it."

"Right." I looked away, conceding, but not really clearing the air.

Margo turned and proceeded into the kitchen. "I'm going to get the salad put together."

"Okay. Let me know if I can help."

We both knew this was a ridiculous offer—I'm worse than helpless in the kitchen, I'm dangerous. Crystal gets broken, bacon gets burned, fires break out. I headed into the den to turn on the TV news; being helpless in the kitchen isn't an entirely bad thing.

My recliner greeted me with a soft whoosh as I settled in. I picked up the remote, but didn't turn on the TV right away. I took comfort in the book-laden shelves, the old-fashioned ordinariness of the braided rug. The smell of garlic and tomato sauce wafted in from the kitchen. I savored a few moments of silence.

Don Dempsey. Was he divorced or wasn't he? Not that it makes any difference. Margo had been divorced a couple of times before I met her and we've been happily married now for twenty years.

The doorbell rang at six o'clock sharp. Well, at least he was prompt. Turns out he's not only prompt, Don Dempsey's a heck of a guy. You know—smart, without being a showoff about it; genial, but not a dispenser of embarrassing horse laughs; and he's kept himself in shape, but isn't a body-builder like Arnold what's-his-face. We all know what that guy was up to when he felt like showing off his rock-hard abs. Margo is the fitness buff in our house—aerobics, Pilates, Zumba—whatever new physical fitness thing comes along, she dives in. As a result, she is in great shape; and me? Not so much. I mean, Michelle Obama wasn't going to come after me in her War Against Obesity…but I could stand to lose a few pounds.

And another thing, Don knows his way around the kitchen.

Margo was all embarrassed because she had told this Don guy six o'clock, never dreaming that he'd actually show up on the dot, and she wasn't quite ready—hadn't sautéed the asparagus or something. So ole Don whips off his suitcoat and rolls up his shirt sleeves and says, "I can do that for you." And he did. I was standing in the doorway kinda watching, ready to give those two some of my expert assistance if it was called for, and he just chopped and sautéed and gave it a little dab of butter, a sprinkle of salt and a squeeze of lemon—all the while keeping up a running reminiscence with Margo about the fun they had back at Franklin High School.

Margo tossed the dressing on the salad, filled up our plates and we went into the dining room to have chicken parmesan on the good dishes. The asparagus was some of the best I've ever had. "Oh, that's because it was good asparagus to start with," Don protested, when Margo and I complimented his culinary skills. "I'll bet you got that at a farmer's market today, didn't you?" he asked, looking at me for some reason.

"As a matter of fact, I picked it up on my way home from the office," I joked—but letting this Don person know that I wasn't completely useless. I held down a job.

Margo blurted out a laugh. "Right. No, that's just straight from the produce section at Safeway," she said. "I think it's your light touch with the sauté pan that made it so good." Alright, now she was overdoing it.

"You certainly have a nice home here." Don changed the subject—and made a nice save, directing his comment to me, the Provider. The dining room did look nice—what with candles glowing on the table and flowers in the middle. I hadn't noticed the flowers 'til just now.

"It's all Margo's doing," I assured him. "I think it's obvious, I'm not much help around the house."

"Inside and out, I mean. I noticed walking up to the front door, your yard looks terrific. Must take a lot of man-hours?"

"Yard service." I stood to refill our glasses with Pinot Grigio—at least I knew how to do that.

"Well, you chose the right service."

"Actually, Margo is responsible for that, too."

Don gave up. "You always were the high achiever," he said to Margo. "Voted 'Most Likely to Succeed,' as I recall. And still in cheerleader shape." Nothing wrong with Don's powers of observation.

Margo had the decency to blush. "I didn't exactly soar to great heights in the career world; but what about you? Sounds as if you're doing well?"

Don had been waiting for this cue; he launched into a narrative about his rise from a nerd in his basement to CEO of one of those computer companies in Silicon Valley. That helped explain why he was wearing jeans with a dress shirt, tie and suit coat—as if he was a TV news anchor.

"Is there more chicken?" I asked, when he paused for breath.

"Help yourself," my otherwise-occupied wife suggested.

"It's fabulous," Don chimed in. "I'd like some more, too, if there's enough."

With that, Margo rose from her chair and reached for both our plates. "I made plenty."

"We'll probably have leftovers tomorrow night," I said.

Margo gave me a look.

"Margo's chicken parmesan is even better warmed up," I hastily pointed out as she left the dining room.

"I may have to see if I can wangle an invitation to come back tomorrow night," Don said, giving me a conspiratorial look. If he thought I was going to do the inviting, he was dead wrong.

I would have thought Margo was out of earshot in the kitchen, but I guess not. She was back at the table in a flash, beaming. "We'd love to have you come back tomorrow night, wouldn't we, George?"

"How long are you in town?" I thought it prudent to ask.

"Just tonight and tomorrow night," Don said. "But I'd be happy to take you folks out for dinner tomorrow night, if there's a restaurant that's a favorite of yours? It'd be good for me to learn a little more about what's happening in town these days—looks like I'll be spending a fair amount of time here over the next couple of months."

"How nice!" Margo exclaimed.

"It's too bad about tomorrow night, though," I said. "I have a school board meeting."

"You're on the school board? Fantastic!" Don seemed genuinely impressed.

"Actually, I'm superintendent of schools, so I really need to be there."

"Wow. Good for you. Margo didn't mention that."

"Well," Margo pointed out, "We really haven't had all that much time for conversation. We still have a lot of catching up to do."

"You're right about that," Don agreed. They both looked at me expectantly. This is where I'm supposed to demonstrate what a generous, trusting husband I am. And ordinarily, I would have said to Margo, "You can go even if I can't." But something about this Don guy made me uncomfortable.

"How about I get your wife out of the kitchen then? You don't mind, do you, George?"

See what I mean? If I object, I'm definitely the one who's the Bad Guy. I decide to pour some more wine, stalling for time. Margo really doesn't need my permission to go off on a dinner *non*-date with an old friend from high school, so this is a sham of an exercise. Might as well play the role of the Good Guy—open-minded, trusting, "with it," whatever that means these days.

"Why don't you go to Esmeralda's?" I suggest, naming the most expensive restaurant I can think of. "Don might as well see how far the old town has come since he's been here last."

Margo beamed. "What a lovely suggestion!"

"Sure you don't mind?" Don asked.

"Of course not," I said. "You two have a lot of catching up to do and I don't think one night's conversation here is going to cover it. I'd like to join you, of course, but that's out of the question—with my School Board meeting and all." Actually, I'd probably be bored stiff and the School Board meeting is providing me with an excellent excuse.

I don't know how she managed it all on such short notice, but Margo even made my favorite dessert—her fabulous apple pie—so this visit from dear old Don was good for something. I even helped her dish it up, putting good-sized scoops of vanilla ice cream on top. I'm good with an ice cream scooper.

Then after dessert, he naturally offered to help clean up—and Margo naturally protested. But Don is a pretty persuasive guy, and Margo was in no hurry to rush him out the door, so in the end she acquiesced and handed Don a dishtowel so he could dry.

"Which one do you want me to use?" I had to ask, pulling open the drawer where I thought the dishtowels might be. Margo gave me a funny look, a kind of silly grin, actually. She was enjoying my not wanting to be one-upped.

"Here," she said, pulling a blue-and-white checked cloth out of the next drawer down and handing it to me. I was glad I asked; that wasn't the one I would have chosen.

We washed and dried and chatted—or rather, Margo and Don chatted. I pretty much maintained a peripheral presence. Margo assigned me the job of putting stuff away when it became obvious Don was a whiz at drying dishes and didn't need an assistant. Eventually, the task was complete and Don decided he had dispensed enough of his charm for one night.

"Sure you won't have an after dinner drink?" I risked asking, determined to match charm for charm, although it was pretty obvious I was going to be outclassed.

He hesitated, making me wish I hadn't been quite so charming.

"Nah, I'd better head out. I've got a big day tomorrow—and a big date tomorrow night!" he said, laughing so I would know he was just joking around.

Yeah, right.

The next morning seems routine enough. Margo halves and sections a grapefruit for us to share and I make my own peanut butter toast.

"I thought the chicken parmesan was a little dry, didn't you?" Margo wants to talk about last night.

"I thought it was great. And Don must have, too. We both had seconds."

"Don was probably just being polite. He's such a gentleman. I can't believe he's the same nerd we locked in the closet in eighth grade Earth Science."

"You locked him in a closet?"

"Kids can do some pretty mean things," she tells me.

Margo seems to forget I'm superintendent of the local school district. This is not unusual—my wife has a proclivity for taking charge of a conversation and directing it to an area where she is an "authority." In her years of chattering away at the breakfast—or dinner—table, it's become obvious where the brains in this family reside.

That bouquet of flowers Don brought to dinner last night has been moved from the dining room to the kitchen island. That's not particularly noteworthy—Margo likes to have flowers in the kitchen. Except that, in this instance, she has merely switched the pot of tulips that were on the island—now relegated to the dining room table—for Don's flowers.

"Nice of Don to bring flowers," I say, rejoining my wife at the kitchen table.

"Yes—I don't know where he found those yellow ranunculus, but they're so beautiful." Margo admires the bouquet on the island for a moment, then pushes back her chair and takes her things to the sink.

"No crossword puzzle this morning?" I ask, noting the newspaper hasn't even been opened.

"I don't have time." Margo hastily rinses her cup and saucer, stashes them in the dishwasher, glancing at the clock on the microwave. "Sandy said she could give me a manicure and a pedicure if I got there right at eight." She grabs her jacket out of the hall closet and in two minutes, she's gone.

It's February and she's going to get a manicure *and a pedicure.* The snow is six inches deep out there—and we aren't going on a cruise, or to her sister's place in Florida. Even I recognize this is not usual, or routine.

A careful silence settles into our little yellow kitchen. I study Don's flowers as I chew on my whole wheat toast. Margo was gone before we had a chance to talk about the two of them having dinner tonight. I had thought about suggesting I join them at Esmeralda's after the school board meeting, just so Don wouldn't think I was being rude. I guess I could play it by ear—see what time the meeting ends and then pop in on them if it's still a reasonable hour.

Or…not.

I pour myself another cup of coffee and unplug the pot. I sit down again at the table, leaf through the newspaper without really absorbing what I read. The quiet is comforting, somehow. Margo is gone, taking her whirlwind of activity with her.

I am alone in the house. And I decide that's not all bad.

Margo

"I think this is a color you'll like," Sandy says, offering Margo a bottle of amber-hued nail polish.

Margo thinks the color is probably right, but turns the bottle over to read the name on the bottom. "*Barefoot in Barcelona.* Perfect!" She hands the bottle back to Sandy, then leans back in the pedicure chair, willing the fragrant hot water bubbling up around her ankles to do its thing. *Take a deep breath,* she told herself. *Take several.* She inhales the soothing scent of spearmint.

Sandy sat on her little stool, busying herself assembling the tools for the pedicure. "Will you want the same color on your fingernails?" she asks.

"Yes, I think so. I'll know for sure after I see it on my toenails."

"Okay." Sandy stands. "Is there anything I can get you? Coffee? Water?"

"No, thanks, I'm good. I've already had my breakfast."

Her pony-tailed nail tech hesitates, then leaves the small back room dedicated to pedicures. Sandy conducts each pedicure according to the wishes of her client—some like to chat continuously throughout the entire procedure, while others prefer this pre-soak period to be a tranquil time. Usually, Margo was eager to chat; today, however, Sandy had somehow been alerted to Margo's wish to be left alone. She needed to think.

Everything had happened in such a whirl. First, Don's phone call early yesterday morning: "I'm about to go into a meeting. I'd have called you last night, but I got in so late," he apologized. "I'm just hoping you, and your husband, are available for dinner tonight. I'd like to do some catching up on the old gang."

Margo had insisted that he come over for a home-cooked meal. And then she wondered—all through the whirlwind of marketing, baking, table-setting, and meal prep, why he had chosen to call *her,* out of all their classmates at Franklin High.

They had never dated in high school, never even been close friends. But then, Don hadn't really had any close friends in all the time she had known him.

Naturally, she wondered if he had harbored a secret crush on her. Why else would he call? And, who had Don become, these thirty years later? All of this became abundantly clear when he arrived for dinner—tall, dark and certainly bordering on handsome—oozing with confidence, and bearing a bouquet of beautiful flowers. The only resemblance to the nerd she remembered was a pair of wire-rimmed glasses that somehow just enhanced the attractiveness of this present-day Don.

And now, she and Don had a dinner date. She knew that, under ordinary circumstances, George would have accompanied them to dinner—it wouldn't be a "date." However, George had a school board meeting. Don couldn't have known that, or planned on it, so why did she think it was a "date?"

Because it felt like one. She was excited. She spent a good deal of time this morning—while George was in the shower—going through her closet, trying to figure out what she should wear. She made a quick phone call to Sandy, and now she was getting a manicure *and a pedicure*.

What did she expect to happen? What did she *want* to happen?

Don

Margo is prettily flushed when she answers the door at six o'clock. Don can see this dinner-date is going to be a slam dunk.

"Do you want a drink?" she asks. As she opens the door and turns to go into the living room, he spies a half-full glass of red wine on the coffee table. Maybe that's the reason for Margo's pink cheeks.

"I'll have whatever you're having," Don says. Which is handy, because the open bottle and another wineglass are sitting there on the coffee table—right next to the flowers he brought to dinner last night. He reaches for the bottle and pours a small amount into the glass.

"To old friends," he says, and clinks his glass with hers. She flushes some more, and takes a healthy gulp of shiraz. He sips, finds it pleasant enough—although a little plummy.

"Don't ever use the word 'old' when you're referring to a woman past a certain age," Margo teases.

"Ah! But we're not old, are we? And I don't know how you manage it, but if I didn't know for sure how old you are—I'd think you were at least ten or fifteen years younger."

"I work at it," she acknowledges. "George doesn't care how old he looks, but I do."

"Well, whatever you're doing, it's working. And that color is great on you. It's not really orange, is it? Would you call that 'coral'?"

"Aren't you sweet?!" Margo's cheeks are beginning to match her silk shirt.

Don glances around the attractive room. There are several framed prints on the walls—although nothing he identifies as an original. Two matching off-white sofas form a conversation area in front of the fireplace, with the coffee table between them. The walls are painted a soft brown—probably called some sort of taupe on the paint chip card. "I'm thinking I may want to get an apartment here in town—would you be willing to help me decorate?"

"Oh, I'd love to!" Margo beams. No one has turned him down on that one yet; it was almost too easy.

"Actually, we'd probably better get going," he says, glancing at his watch. "Our reservation at Esmeralda's is for six-thirty."

He replaces his wineglass on the coffee table. Margo drains hers and sets it down next to his, then reaches for the coat lying over the arm of the couch nearest the door.

The conversation at dinner centers on the good old days at Franklin High. With scarcely a prompt from Don, Margo launches into reminiscing about the excitement of the state basketball championship of their senior year—it seemed her cheerleading had somehow contributed greatly to the team's success. She assumes Don was in attendance at all the tournament games—wasn't everybody? Ah, but nerdy little Don was not. He had to work every weekend plus a couple of nights a week bagging groceries at the supermarket, saving every penny he earned to help pay for college. But it was apparent from this discussion that—just as he guessed—his presence hadn't been missed.

Things were going just as he planned. And Don was going to make sure Margo missed "the little nerd" the next time around.

Margo

Margo scrubbed her elbows with pumice stone, lathered her body in expensive apricot-scented body wash, and inspected her pedicure to make sure it still looked good. She was so thankful she had put in the hours and hours demanded each week on the Stairmaster to keep her body in good shape. Not many women her age could look at their nude selves in a full-length mirror and be satisfied—but Margo could. And now she planned to unveil her beautifully-toned body to Don Dempsey.

She made this decision while she was lying in bed this morning—wide awake at five o'clock—despite the fact that she had way too much wine at dinner the night before. Her husband George was gently snoring beside her as she weighed the pros and cons of violating their marriage vows for the first time ever. And she decided it was worth the risk.

"Why don't we have lunch tomorrow?" Don suggested last night at dinner at Esmeralda's. "If it's not too inconvenient, how about that restaurant at my hotel? I'll be leaving town late in the afternoon—it'll give us one last chance to get to know one another better. To become reacquainted."

She knew what lunch at a man's hotel meant. She was no babe in the woods. Nor was she too old to play this game.

So Margo dressed carefully in a soft turquoise sweater and skirt. Even George had commented on what a good color that was for her. And pretty matching silk underwear.

She didn't want to appear too eager, so she planned to arrive a few minutes late. Even so, the hostess said, "Mr. Dempsey isn't here yet. But I can seat you."

The attractive young thing with lots of décolletage led Margo to a table in a remote corner of the restaurant. Margo was sure Don had given instructions for a "quiet table." There was even a potted ficus parked right in front of the table. He was being so discreet.

She decided to order a glass of wine. Don would probably be here by the time the wine arrived. The waiter promptly delivered her glass of pinot grigio. Margo breathed in its lovely crispness, then sipped. She carefully studied her surroundings—strategically placed mirrors made the room appear larger than it actually was. She knew that trick—perhaps she'd suggest it for Don's apartment. The tile floor looked a little tacky, Margo much preferred hardwood—oak or even pine. She sipped her wine some more. Perused the menu. Checked her makeup in her purse mirror. And waited. Don must have been detained by some business deal.

When the overly solicitous waiter asked if she would care to order, she said, "No, I'll wait."

She ordered a second glass of wine—telling herself not to get so pie-eyed she wouldn't be able to remember this afternoon's activities. She tried taking tiny sips.

"Is there any message from Mr. Dempsey?" she asked, when the waiter again suggested she might wish to order.

"No, ma'am, I'm afraid there's not." His look seemed to say *you are a stupid, foolish old woman who has been stood up.*

After another half-hour of waiting, she decided he was right.

Margo stumbled a little on the steps leaving the restaurant, but saved herself from a fall by clutching the railing so thoughtfully provided.

George

Margo is definitely subdued this morning. It's not difficult to decipher—she's *quiet*. When Margo is quiet the whole house is quiet. Drawers open and close discreetly on silent gliders, silverware settles softly into place at the table, even the coffee maker carefully masks the usual noisy crescendo at the completion of its task. This is Margo's domain, it follows her direction. And although I am suspicious of the reason for her subdued state, I like the quiet. Thank you, Don.

For I am certain it is Don Dempsey we have to thank for this quietude. He was here, now he's gone. I had yet another meeting last night so Margo was in bed, supposedly asleep, when I came home; I have not had a report on their lunch together. Now, either Margo is plotting to run away with him and is thus overwhelmingly preoccupied, or his visit has somehow gone awry and this is a Disappointed Quiet.

"Coffee?" I ask—the first words spoken between us this morning. While I am pretty much useless in the kitchen, I do know how to make a pot of coffee and am about to pour the first cup.

"Yes, please." Margo is sitting at her place, her face expressionless.

I pour her a cup and deliver it—black—to the kitchen table, where she unfolds the newspaper as if she were a programmed robot.

I dump cream and sugar into my cup and settle into my chair, easing the front section of the paper away from Margo, who is staring at the LIFE section with unseeing eyes.

The rest of the world seems to be in pretty good shape—unemployment claims here are down, the euro is reportedly stabilized, and there are signs our sanctions are having the desired effect on North Korea.

"I think I'll make bacon and eggs," Margo announces, pushing back her chair and standing. "Do you want some?"

"Do we even have any bacon?"

"Yes, I bought some for the salad. Do you want some or not?"

"Sure." Only a fool would turn down bacon and eggs. "You want me to make the toast?"

"I can handle it," she says, and I can tell by the sound of the skillet being slammed onto the stovetop that the Quiet Time is over.

Margo doesn't have to ask *how* I want my eggs, but she does ask, "Two eggs or three?"

Who's in Charge Here, Anyway?

-1-

Sid took one of the good dinner plates from the china cabinet. He filled it with Purina's Vibrant Maturity dog food and set it on the floor, where Chuckles waited patiently. Sid felt Louise's disapproval, even though she had been dead for nearly a year. Of course she would object to his using her fancy china to feed the dog—but what else was it good for these days? Neither of his daughters wanted it; they had their own dishes and glasses and crockpots, booty from long-ago wedding registries.

He sat down at the kitchen table to watch Chuckles go at it. "Good stuff, eh, Chuckles?"

The old yellow Lab looked up briefly at the mention of his name, rheumy brown eyes puzzled by the interruption, then went back to licking the plate clean.

"We're a pair, you and me, Chuckles," Sid said. "Bachelors again, but without the wherewithal to get into much trouble." Chuckles moved over to his water dish and began noisily lapping away, splashing water in a wide arc on the kitchen floor.

Sid realized he forgot to put down the brown rug that he usually kept under the water dish. Was this a sign of impending dementia, or just routine absentmindedness? He wasn't used to not being on top of things.

Over the course of forty-two years with Gilberts Tool & Die, Sid had worked himself up to general manager. He knew he'd never be CEO—that job belonged to Peter Gilberts III—but Sid was, for all practical purposes, in charge of the whole kit and caboodle. And he liked that responsibility—that power. So it was with some reluctance that he had relinquished the day-to-day managerial duties and assumed the role of part-time consultant. But he felt he was needed at home.

It had been a shock when he realized there was something seriously wrong with Louise—something more than "routine absentmindedness." She seemed fine; actually, she was in very good physical shape for a woman of seventy-two, and that's probably why it took so long for Sid and his daughters to catch on. He should have known something was amiss when Louise stopped reaching for the newspaper's crossword puzzle when she sat down with her morning coffee.

Finally there was the day she came home from the grocery store—ashen and looking frail, uncertain.

"I missed the turn off Broadway, and I got lost," she announced. She stood inside the screen door, the groceries still in the car, and looked at her husband of forty-eight years.

"I got lost coming home from Trader Joe's, Sid."

He went to her and took her in his arms to comfort her. Louise broke away and collapsed into her favorite armchair, plainly shaken.

"What's happening to me?"

Louise's lucidity deteriorated painfully over the next three years, until the time came when she didn't recognize her daughters and sometimes didn't even know Sid's name. One day she had called him "Henry"—whoever the hell that was.

Despite a daily routine that grew more and more frustrating, Sid had felt good about his role as chief caretaker—about being needed again. His usefulness as a sexual partner had taken a big hit when his doctor prescribed that drug for his high blood pressure a few years back. Louise didn't seem to mind—but it made him feel inadequate at home. Fortunately, at that time he was still in charge at Gilberts, so he didn't feel entirely worthless. At the plant, 50—even 60 or more hours a week, he had still been the go-to guy.

Sid knew one thing—the thought of losing it mentally scared the shit out of him. Was it his turn now? Did it matter if you ate blueberries and worked crossword puzzles? Frank, down the street, was ninety and the sole sum of his exercise was a stroll to the corner bar every afternoon for his four o'clock martini. He was sharp as a tack.

Sid realized he might reach a point, as Louise had, where he wasn't even aware of his "condition"—wouldn't even care. But what about his girls? Should they have to go through something like that all over again?

Did he really not have any control over when he died? And how?

-2-

I watch Sid get up from the kitchen table, pushing with his right arm and then pausing a minute to steady himself. Sid hasn't had his morning coffee yet. Maybe that's what he's getting up to do—it would make moving around easier, even a dog knows that.

"Well, I'm up," Sid announces. "What was I gonna do?" He looks to me for his answer. I go over to the kitchen counter and stand where the coffeepot is. I wag my tail. I'd bark, but that might be a bit much for the situation. Clearly, this is not a life-saving Lassie moment.

"Might as well make some coffee, long as I'm up. Okay, Chuckles?"

I sit. He got the message.

Sid and I have been together a long time and by and large Sid has treated me right. I guess I'm mellowing as I near eighty-four in dog years; I'm nearly ready to forgive Sid for naming me "Chuckles." Louise, bless her dearly-departed soul, had wanted to name me "Charlie," which would have been fine. But *Chuckles*? C'mon. Imagine trying to impress the fancy lady dogs in the neighborhood with a moniker like *Chuckles*.

The kitchen begins to fill with the aroma of fresh coffee as Sid puts a couple of pieces of whole wheat bread in the toaster.

Sid probably thought Louise wanted to name me Charlie in honor of some old boyfriend. I don't know if that was the case or not, but Louise sure was a charmer. Sid wasn't too swift in that department; he never did seem to catch on about Louise and Hank, that landscaper guy. I liked Hank; he always brought a nice meaty bone for me to gnaw on while he and Louise dilly-dallied upstairs. I wasn't allowed in the house with a bone, so they knew I'd be otherwise occupied outside for a certain length of time.

Louise preferred to call him by his given name. "'Henry' suits you so much better," she'd say, patting him on the cheek. But I noticed she always referred to him as Hank when she discussed lawn care with Sid.

Then Hank had a heart attack and died—not while he was dilly-dallying upstairs, fortunately. That's about when Louise began to slow down. It was sad to watch, especially because it upset Sid's equilibrium so.

But I think he's made a nice recovery in the last few months. So what if he uses the good dishes for my dog food? It's actually kind of sweet that he thinks I'm that special.

In return, I keep an eye on him—the daughters know that, so they let Sid stay here in the house instead of shipping him off to a nursing home. And that kind of safeguards me against any attempt to "put me down" prematurely. I'm not eager to go; but I don't want to hang around past my useful-ness, either. I'm depending on Sid to send me to doggie heaven before things get unbearably sloppy. Wish I could make the same promise to him. Me and Sid, we're a team.

-3-

The patio was always my favorite spot, even before Henry did all that beautiful landscaping. I sat here with my cup of coffee and listened as the sun woke the birds in the morning. Much later in the day, with a glass of anything red, I kept track of the quail scurrying about and watched darkness slide in across the valley and creep up the Catalinas.

Now that I'm of the spirit world, I can sit wherever I want, for as long as I want. And I still spend a lot of time here on my little patio. Sid prefers watching the ballgame and his game shows on TV to being out-of-doors; if it weren't for Chuckles, I don't know if he'd ever get out. Thank god for that dog—being Sid's constant companion was wearing me out. Getting a dog for him was a stroke of genius, if I do say so myself, even if it is more than a little irritating to watch Sid use my good china for a dog dish.

Don't get me wrong, I loved Sid with all my heart, still do. But the silly nincompoop took togetherness to the ex-treme, which—after he retired—nearly drove me crazy. Come to think of it, maybe it did.

Sorry, guess that's not fair. But things were manageable while Sid had to go off to work every day and I had some time to myself. When he went into semi-retirement mode, I suggested we make a visit to the dog pound and we found this wonderful yellow Lab puppy. They bonded immediately, Sid and Chuckles, and they're still taking care of one another.

The problem is, they're both getting to the age when they have to pee more often, so Chuckles always wants to go out, and Sid wants to stay in—near the toilet.

Sid is winning that battle this afternoon, with "Jeopardy" blaring away and Chuckles lying at his feet. At this rate, they're both just going to get stiffer in the joints. Instead of sitting here feeling sorry for themselves—wondering when they're going to die, why don't they go with Frank for a four o'clock martini?

I learned early on that Chuckles is more responsive to messages from the spirit world than Sid is. So I'm not surprised now when Chuckles cranks himself up and gets his leash, then stands in front of the TV so Sid has no choice but to click it off and head for the door.

As luck would have it—*riiight*—Frank is just coming down his walk, brandishing that fancy cane of his, when Sid and Chuckles approach his place. Frank pats Chuckles on the head.

"Chuckles looks good, Sid. How about you? How are you doing?"

"We're both doing well, Frank, thanks. How about you?"

Frank nods. "Same old, same old."

Here's where Sid comes up with, "If it ain't broke, don't fix it."

Frank takes a step down the walk, stops, then turns. "Care to join me? Chuckles will be okay if we sit on the Hacienda's patio."

I hold my breath a minute, wondering if Sid is up to this spur-of-the-moment invitation.

"Don't mind if we do. Thanks, Frank."

-4-

Now this is more like it—Sid and me, out amongst 'em. It was very sporting of Frank to invite us to join him for a drink at the Hacienda. There aren't any other dogs here, which is actually all right with me. And it's nice on the shady patio with pots of cactus all around; you want to stay away from those things though, backing into one can hurt like heck.

Sid is obviously enjoying himself; he seems quite oblivious to the time—doesn't even realize that it's almost 4:30 and time for "The Price Is Right." It's good for Sid to hang out with Frank. He's been doing okay since Louise passed away, but Sid does have those troublesome lapses into self-absorption that border on pity parties. You can see him stewing in his own juices, wondering what's ahead and if he's going to end up all befuddled like Louise did.

"I expect you still have your lonely moments," Frank says to Sid now. "Your Louise was always so charming—you must miss her." He raises his martini toward Sid, who responds by clinking his Bud Light bottle with Frank's glass.

"Yeah, she was a special lady," Sid agrees. "And our marriage worked—sometimes we had to make little accommodations—but it worked for each of us in our own way."

Whoa! Is he saying what I think he's saying? I may have been underestimating old Sid here big-time. Sounds as if he was way ahead of both me and Louise.

"But you know, toward the end," Sid continues, "Louise wasn't herself. It was kind of scary."

"Scary for you, maybe," Frank says. "But was Louise scared?"

Sid thinks for a minute. "Maybe in the beginning. But then she seemed okay, actually. Happy in her own little world. Usually she knew me, but sometimes she thought I was somebody else. Whoever she thought I was, she liked when I would sit and talk with her about any little thing, hold her hand."

"You were good to her, Sid."

"I didn't do any more than any other husband would have. But it made me feel useful. I miss that, Frank," Sid says. Now we're in for a bit of the contemplative Sid.

"Do you ever wonder why we're allowed to live beyond our ability to feel worthwhile?" I can see him getting a little teary-eyed and I get up and change positions, just to distract him, lighten the mood.

"Well, you still have Chuckles here to take care of," Frank says, right on cue.

"I don't know who's taking care of whom," Sid says. He manages a weak smile as he leans over to give me a pat.

"That's kind of a nice arrangement then, isn't it?" Frank says, smiling back at Sid.

"I guess..." Sid looks at me somewhat dubiously, so I get up and stretch, then stand at his knee with my best patient-dog look. Sid takes the hint.

"Well, we better get a little more walk in, get the kinks out." Sid drains his beer. "Thanks for the invite."

"You're welcome to join me anytime," Frank says. "I appreciate the company."

Sid and I head on down around the block. I like this part of the walk—this is the busy street—the side of the block that has the cleaners, the donut shop, and the branch library that's on the corner at the other end. There's always more activity; people coming and going. I think Sid kind of likes it, too.

Sometimes people make a comment about me—"what a nice dog"—they'll say, and Sid smiles as if he's responsible.

A couple of women are standing talking outside the library, each hanging onto the arm of a little kid. Now another lady comes out with a toddler asleep in a stroller—the afternoon Story Hour must be over. The first two ladies are whispering and cooing over the tyke in the stroller. It's actually kind of congested as we try to make our way around the bunch of them without going into the street.

Woof! That's when Sid turns into Superman.

-5-

It all happened so fast. I know they always say that, but it did. One minute Chuckles and I are minding our own business, making our way down the sidewalk outside the library, and all of a sudden there's this little kid out in the street. I let go of Chuckles' leash—without even consciously making a choice, as I think about it later—and dashed out there to get the little bugger before he was flattened by one of those big SUV's coming around the corner. I don't know if the driver saw the kid, but he sure as heck saw me and slammed on his brakes, making a terrible screeching noise, but without actually making contact with either the boy or me. Chuckles started barking up a storm but had sense enough to stay on the sidewalk, and I was back there in a split-second with a terrified, screaming Austin. Turns out that's what the boy's name is. Austin. Sounds like somebody from one of those PBS movies Louise liked to watch.

Austin's mom let out one yelp, then realized that her primary responsibility at this moment was going to be to calm Austin. She gathered him up and began that shushing that parents spend a lot of time doing. "Shhh-hhh-h, shh-hh-h. It's okay. You're okay."

Austin is blubbering, but he's not screaming anymore. The SUV driver is all shook up and gets out of his vehicle and starts hollering at the mom—"Lady, you need to do a better job of keeping track of your kid. I coulda killed him!"

I get hold of Chuckles' leash and then walk over to the guy. "Luckily, everybody's okay. You obviously were driving within the speed limit and were able to stop." He quits hollering and looks at me, still taking big gulps of air. I say, a little quieter, "That mother is feeling bad enough without you yelling at her."

He looks at Austin's mom, who is still clinging to the boy and continuing the shushing. Austin is probably four or five years old—I'm not good at guessing the ages of kids anymore—but he's a big armful for his mom.

"Is he okay?" the driver asks, now much subdued. "I mean, I can take you to the E.R. or a doctor's office, if you need to go there."

"He's just scared," says one of the other mothers, she has her hand resting on Austin's mom's shoulder.

"Thank you," says Austin's mom. Her name turns out to be Samantha. "Thank you for stopping in time. I think…" her eyes are still widened with the terror of what might have been. "I think we'll be okay."

"I didn't even see him," says the driver. "But I did see *him*"—and he turns to point at me.

Chuckles barks at the driver—SUV drivers are not permitted to point at his master.

"Thank god," says the woman with her hand on Samantha's shoulder. There's a murmured assent among the little crowd that has gathered. Chuckles senses their approval and backs up against me, proudly sitting on my foot to claim me as his own.

I'm a little proud, too. I didn't know I had it in me.

Samantha struggles to hold onto Austin while sticking out one hand to me. "Yes," she says. "Thank you so very much for rescuing Austin. I'm Samantha Fitzgerald. You must be our guardian angel."

Now I'm flustered, but I manage to shake her hand. Her son turns to peer at me while still having his head planted firmly in the crook of his mother's shoulder. His tears have dampened her pink dress. "This is Austin," Samantha says.

"Sid Marcus," I respond. "And this is Chuckles." Which, of course, prompts another bark. Austin looks interested. Kids have always liked Chuckles—and he likes them. Austin attempts to reach down to pat Chuckles while still clinging to his mother, but he can't quite reach, so Samantha gently, slowly, lowers her son to his feet. His face is still red, but his tears are drying. While maintaining a firm grip on his mother's leg with one hand, he manages to pat Chuckles on his backside with the other.

She watches her son pet my dog and takes a deep breath, gives her shoulders a twist and a stretch, then meets my gaze. "It's a good thing you were here, Sid Marcus," Samantha says.

To Lego or Not

Carrie chose the bright blue bra from her lingerie drawer and then the matching panties—a set Cliff had given her when their relationship was new. She knew the blue bra strap would be visible through her crocheted white top but that was the whole idea of flirty underwear, wasn't it?

Cliff's wife didn't wear pretty lingerie; she wore old-lady-white underpants. That's what Cliff called them. Carrie secretly wondered if his wife might wear sexy underthings if he would surprise her with such a gift, but she wasn't about to suggest it.

Freshly showered and seductively scented, Carrie was a fit and sturdy redhead who wore her hair short and curly. She returned to the kitchen where the aroma of vegetables roasting in the oven suggested she might open the bottle of good pinot noir even before Cliff arrived. But what if he brought a bottle? Would he be disappointed that she had begun their evening without him? Ah, well—Cliff was a big boy. There was that lovely pop as she pulled the cork from the bottle, then poured just a little into her glass. She was only making sure it would be right with the salmon.

The table looked beautiful—the plates were dark red Fiestaware, almost burgundy. The salmon would look so pretty on these plates, as would the vegetables. Some men could care less about a table setting, but Carrie had discovered Cliff respected her talent for food prep and presentation. It was how she made her living—a much less hectic way of life than that of chef in one of the fanciest restaurants downtown, which is what she had been doing when she met Cliff. Tonight marked the one year anniversary of their first "date."

Being head chef at Narcissus paid well, but it was an emotional roller coaster and it also meant she worked late into the evening and was exhausted when she left the restaurant. So Cliff encouraged her to start her own business—a food blog. He even bankrolled her startup; they both called it an "investment," that also made it possible for their relationship to bloom and flourish.

Carrie moved the bowl of orange tulips just a skosh. That was one of the idiosyncrasies of dating a married man—in her case, at least. She really had to provide her own flowers. What if he ran into someone he knew at the flower shop? Or heading down the street to her place with flowers in hand? Without the flowers, he could make up any sort of story, but with flowers—that made it awkward.

It was okay, she enjoyed picking out her own flowers and had bunches throughout the apartment.

"I like coming here with flowers everywhere," Cliff told her. "So much nicer than stepping over Legos in every room."

Of course there were Legos all over his house; every time Cliff went on a trip he brought back a new set. Even when the "conference" was actually a romantic rendezvous with Carrie, they made the mandatory stop in the airport gift shop to purchase Legos. It seemed all three of his kids—two boys and a girl—loved building things and were creative geniuses.

The salmon was good—lightly crusted with Dijon mustard and then baked for just twelve minutes. It was the perfect dish for those rare occasions when Cliff could come for dinner because she just popped it in the oven whenever he arrived. So they had it often, but Cliff didn't seem to mind.

And no dessert. One didn't want to be stuffed when sex was on the agenda. Just the rest of the bottle of wine after they had cleared the table. Cliff always helped; Carrie felt it was his way of "playing house." She wondered—and even asked—"Do you clear the table at home?"

"No, it's one of the chores we've given the kids. I used to, but now the two older ones take the dishes to the kitchen. It's good for them to learn some responsibility."

They settled on her couch with half-full glasses of the pinot noir. "Good choice," Cliff commented. "One of your many talents."

"It's part of my job," she pointed out.

He set down his glass and leaned over to kiss her lightly. Her top slid off one shoulder and he reached for the bra strap. "Good color on you." He pulled that nearly naked shoulder toward him.

Carrie put her glass down and kissed him back. She liked that he appreciated the way she dressed, her deliberately provocative way of tempting him. Not that he needed tempting. And the sex was always good.

"Where are you supposed to be tonight?" Carrie asked as he eased himself out of her bed afterward.

"Dinner with Jacobs," Cliff replied, naming a client.

He was gone by 9:30.

Which didn't bother Carrie at all. Another woman might have cried herself to sleep when her lover left to go home to his wife. But Carrie turned on the TV to catch up on "Dancing With the Stars"—which Cliff would have deemed silly. Maybe she just liked having her place to herself.

Her cell phone jangled on her bedside table a little after midnight. "CLIFF" it said.

"She's gone." Carrie scarcely recognized his distraught voice.

"Who's gone?"

"Sandy. My wife, Sandy. She's left me."

"Just now?"

"Yes. Just now. She was waiting for me when I got home and wanted to know where I'd been."

"Didn't you tell her you had a meeting with whatshis-name—Jacobs?"

"I did. But apparently Jacobs called here looking for me while I was supposedly with him."

"Oh, Cliff." Carrie really thought he was smarter than that—would have considered all the possibilities when making up an alibi.

"We had a terrible fight. She was really angry. I thought she was gonna throw something at me."

"But she didn't?"

"No. She kept crying and making me answer all these questions and not even giving me a chance to answer."

"What would you have said?" Carrie plumped up a pillow in back of her against the headboard.

"Oh, I don't know, something. But I didn't even have time to think of anything. She...she had a suitcase all packed and just walked out the door. I couldn't believe it."

"What did you think she would do when she found out?"

Silence.

"Cliff?"

"I guess I didn't think she would find out."

Right. And the moon is made of green cheese.

"Where are the kids?" Carrie asked, trying to picture the scene.

"Oh, they're upstairs. Asleep, I think. It was a very quiet, very intense argument. A lot of hissing. I could tell Sandy didn't want to wake them."

"Well, that's good, at least."

"Yeah, so they're good. But I'm not so good. This has been quite a shock."

"I can imagine," Carrie sympathized.

"So, could you come over?"

She wasn't sure she heard him correctly—shifted the phone to her other ear.

"What?"

"Could you come over? Help me figure out what to do?"

"Cliff…"

"You're always so good at logistics and…"

"That is definitely not a good idea, Cliff."

"But what am I gonna do? I have to get to the office tomorrow, and the kids have to get to school. Sandy always makes sure they get up and have breakfast, and that's usually after I'm gone. I have an 8:30 meeting." He paused to take a breath and sighed. "This is gonna screw up my whole day."

"Your whole *day?*" Carrie repeated.

"You know what I mean. I have to get a handle on things."

"Here's what you're going to do, Cliff. You'll call the office first thing and reschedule the 8:30. You'll get the kids up and tell them their mother's sister is ill in Buffalo or some such thing and then give them breakfast and get them off to school. Then you'll call your lawyer. Because, Cliff, your wife is going to come back. She's not going to leave her kids. She'll return and then she's going to tell you to leave and then she's probably going to file for divorce. So you better have your ducks in a row."

"When do you think she'll come back?" Cliff asked.

"I don't know that, Cliff. It may be tomorrow, it may be next week. Does she have her own credit cards?"

"What if I don't leave? She can't make me leave, can she?"

"Is that what you want?" Carrie wondered.

"But where would I go?" She could almost see him grimace. "One of those extended stay places where all the kicked-out husbands go?"

"That wouldn't be so bad, temporarily."

"I could come stay with you…"

"No, Cliff. You couldn't. Not now. Not six months from now. Not ever."

She hated kicking a guy when he was down, but …

Picking Up the Pieces

Deep in a daydream, Janet almost launched into "Take Me Out to the Ballgame" instead of "Lamb of God" at Communion. That would have been embarrassing. As it was, she saw Father John glance up at her in the choir loft—he heard that first errant note before she recovered, remembered where she was.

Which was at the organ for eight o'clock Mass at St. Seraphina's Catholic Church, just hours away from her shift as a Guest Services Ambassador at Wrigley Field. These two occupations were not to be confused, although both were performed in what Janet regarded as rarefied air.

Janet loved to bring the entire congregation to its feet with a hymn that resounded through this beautiful old church in Chicago's K-Town. Dust mites mingled in the sunlight streaming through the stained-glass windows; the smell of old wood and a trace of incense hung in the air. The ten o'clock Mass featured music provided by a trio of Spanish guitars, but this early Mass was traditional, old school—with the kind of music that had been played for decades in St. Seraphina's. No choir now, granted. Just Janet, creating majestic music befitting the solemnity of Sunday Mass.

As soon as Mass was over she would duck into the ladies' room and change into her Cubs' blue, tucking her fifteen extra pounds under the loose-fitting jersey and her still-auburn curls under her "C" cap. She made a bee-line for the CTA stop at Pulaski and 21st and caught the Pink Line north. It took about an hour to get to Wrigley Field—transferring to the Red Line along the way—but she always arrived in plenty of time to check in and then begin greeting the enthusiastic fans arriving early for Cubs baseball. This was the best job ever. Sure, some people got a little testy when you had to make them move because they weren't in the right seats— she could nominate many for Academy Awards the way they feigned surprise that their tickets weren't for Section 131, but for Section 431.

But how about being part of all the excitement at Wrigley? The Cubs were having the best year they'd had in a long time, certainly the best since she'd started ushering—'scuse me, greeting patrons as a Guest Services Ambassador. And she worked the section above first base, where that cutie pie Anthony Rizzo performed his magic. She was right there to see him climb the rail and perch atop the rolled up canvas to catch that fly ball. And she got paid to be there! Well, granted, not that much—but she didn't have to fork over the big bucks that people who bought tickets did. Her favorites were the Friday afternoon games—sunshine, green grass, the smell of those kosher dogs on the grill. So what if it had been over a hundred years since the Cubs had won the World Series?

Janet had not been working at Wrigley all that long. It was a much coveted job among seniors—and Janet was only sixty-one. But her regular job during the week was in the office of St. Seraphina's School, so she had the summers off anyway and decided about ten years ago to look into the possibility of being a Wrigley Field usher. The season started before school was out, of course, and then extended into September (and

October if they were lucky!) after school started up again. But the heaviest attendance coincided with Janet's summer off, and she had no trouble working the minimum number of games in order to guarantee being hired back the next year.

This year, there'd been no problem at all because there was no St. Seraphina's School anymore. It was just one of the many schools the diocese had to close because there weren't enough kids to fill the classrooms. So Janet joined the ranks of the retired, a few years earlier than she planned.

Luckily, she didn't have to pay rent or a mortgage payment. Her parents had bought their 2-flat before Janet was even born, living downstairs and renting out the upstairs apartment to help make the mortgage payment. It was a good deal then, and although the neighborhood had changed some since, it was certainly a good deal for Janet. She lived alone; her mom had died young—younger than Janet was now, come to think of it. Then her dad died just about ten years ago, after more than a few years of Janet caring for him, taking him to doctors' appointments, cooking their evening meal. After he passed is when she decided to become a Cubs usher, when she suddenly found herself with lots of free time in the summers.

"Now with the school closed, I have lots of free time in the winter," Janet remarked to Frieda, one of the other ushers. "I can only stand to watch so much TV."

"You need to get yourself a hobby," Frieda said. "My sister and I took a knitting class together and now I'm knitting up a storm all winter long. It's good therapy."

"I don't see myself as a knitter."

Frieda shrugged and turned to the couple coming up the steps, "May I see your tickets, please?"

What Janet really wanted was to be the full-time organist at Wrigley Field. She knew she had every bit as much musical talent as Gary Pressy, sitting high up in his booth above home plate, playing "Good Vibrations" when Anthony Rizzo came up to bat, "Bailondo" when Miggy Montero approached the batter's box. Wasn't it time for someone new up there? Like Janet? She could dream.

When October came and the Cubs weren't in the World Series again that year, Janet saw a flyer at the grocery store for classes at the art supply store near the Pink Line station. Maybe she'd just stop in and look around.

That's how she found herself gluing little pieces of ceramic tile to a plate in November. There were a half-dozen women in the mosaic tile class, some with plans to create Christmas gifts; others—like Janet—wanted to do something artistic without necessarily being able to draw or paint. With a great deal of help from their instructor, who was also the store owner, Janet created a plate with a deep green background and a pretty white dove. Christmas-y. And not bad for her first effort.

The store provided all the supplies for their first projects, but then Janet and her classmates were advised they might want to begin to acquire some of their own materials. Over the winter months Janet spent a lot of time browsing at flea markets and tag sales, rummaging through her own attic. She spread the word among her siblings—her two married sisters and her one sister-in-law—that she'd be happy to take off their hands any cast-offs: odd plates, saucers, leftover squares of ceramic tile from bathroom or kitchen remodeling jobs. Preferably solid-colored. Flat pieces were better than curved, but she could make some of the slightly rounded pieces from mugs or vases work.

Janet wasn't quite sure what her next project would be, but she wanted to have raw product on hand for when the inspiration struck her.

In the meantime, she snuck into St. Seraphina's on weekday afternoons when nobody was around to practice ballpark songs on the organ. She had "Take Me Out to the Ballgame" and "Go Cubs Go" down pat, but wanted to work on the other songs that a savvy Wrigley Field musician might play to entertain the crowd on a sunny day in what Steve Goodman called "that ivy-covered burial ground." You never know, Gary Pressy might have a heart attack and keel over. Somebody had to be ready to step in. Janet was determined to be that somebody.

"Hey, Janet, are the Cubs coming to Mass Sunday?"

Janet nearly jumped out of her skin. There was Father John, right behind her, grinning from ear to ear.

"Oh, sorry, Father."

"Hope I didn't scare you?"

"No, no. Well, maybe a little. I wasn't aware anyone else was in the church."

"I heard the music when I left the rectory next door and thought I'd better stop in to check it out," the genial priest told her.

"Sorry, Father."

"No need to apologize. It's probably good for the organ to get used now and then between Sundays."

"It probably is," Janet was quick to agree. "I was going to start practicing some of the music for next Sunday's mass next."

"Right." Father John looked at her a little quizzically.

"It's so cold out, I thought a little baseball park music might warm things up." Janet was grasping for some sort of explanation.

"Aha! Next thing you know I'll be hearing luau music," he beamed at her. "Should I go get my ukulele?"

She laughed. "I didn't know you were a musician, Father John."

"I'd have to get myself to Confession if I said I was, Janet. I don't really have a ukulele—I was just kidding. You'll forgive me, won't you?"

Janet could feel her face redden. She issued a strangled giggle.

"Not to worry," Father John said. "There's no sin in a feeble joke. I apologize for interrupting your practice session. I'll be off." The priest patted her on the shoulder and then was off down the steep steps from the choir loft, whistling "Take Me Out to the Ballgame" as he descended.

She waited until she heard him go out the heavy front door, then opened the hymnal on the music stand and launched into "Soon and Very Soon," one of her favorite recessional hymns.

Later, as she was in the kitchen warming up last night's goulash, Janet wondered if she felt more guilty about getting caught playing baseball music on the church organ, or about her half-heartedly wishing some mishap might befall Gary Pressy. Maybe her wish was even more than half-hearted. She couldn't recall ever wishing real harm to anyone before.

Except maybe Bruce Osinski, that painter she had hired a half-dozen years ago to paint the entire upstairs apartment between renters. He had flirted shamelessly with Janet to the extent that she daydreamed about giving up her virginity— along with her spinsterhood, of course—until someone at school told her he had a wife and four little Osinskis at home. Janet considered two possibilities: murder Osinski by sticking his head in a paint bucket, or joining the convent. Within a week, the painting job was done, Bruce Osinski was gone, and she returned to the safety of life as usual.

Just thinking about that painter person sent Janet to the corner of the basement where she hammered plates to pieces.

The long-neglected ping-pong table was her work space. She donned her safety glasses and chose a pretty turquoise dinner plate from the cardboard box on the floor. She set the plate face down on the old blanket she used to cushion the blows, picked up her hammer and BAM! smashed the plate right in the middle. That first blow was always the best. Janet wasn't crazy about the grouting part, but she loved the smashing part. The blanket helped keep the pieces on the table, which she proceeded to hammer into smaller and smaller pieces until she had chips suitably sized for ceramic tile work.

Only one plate tonight. This was exhausting work, and although Janet was in good shape, the Cardinals were coming to town tomorrow and there'd be a big crowd at the ballpark.

Friday afternoon at Wrigley, the wind blowing out. "There must be forty-thousand here today, don't you think?" Frieda speculated.

"It's always this way with the Cardinals," Janet agreed. It was the top of the seventh and the Cardinals were up 4-3. Many of the Guest Services Ambassadors found themselves with little to do. Janet made her way up toward the organist's perch—she wanted to see Gary Pressy accompany the guest conductor— some hockey player she'd never heard of—in singing "Take Me Out to the Ballgame" in the seventh inning stretch.

Pressy looked disgustingly healthy. If she was going to wait for him to drop over from a heart attack, she'd have a very long wait. Janet knew he took good care of himself, worked out daily, even took the stairs all the way up to his organist's booth instead of the elevator. She had to admire the way he led the hockey player--who had no voice at all, by the way—and the crowd, with the right pace so everybody could keep up. It was a highlight of every game; they really didn't need some no-name celebrity to "lead" the crowd.

When the song ended, Pressy got up and looked as if he was going to leave his perch—something he rarely did during a game. Maybe he needed a bathroom break. Janet was close enough to the door to the booth; she could reach out and touch him if she wanted. Or she could stick her foot out and see what happened. Maybe Pressy would fall to the cement steps and get one of those concussions everybody is suddenly talking about. Wouldn't that be a shame? After the medics hauled him away, she'd be right there. Nobody would suspect her, and she could just slide in there on the organist's bench and finish playing for the rest of the game.

The next day they'd come to her and ask her to finish out the season.

Janet glanced down at the grassy green field which would become her domain. She saw Anthony Rizzo taking practice swings in the on-deck circle and realized he was up next. He could hit a homer and tie up the game.

But he probably wouldn't if she tripped Pressy and created a scene. A distraction. A jinx. A new Chicago Cubs Curse.

Janet turned and descended to her place in the right-field stands. She didn't know if Pressy even ever left the booth, maybe he was just stretching.

That night she found a small vase in her basement stash that was just the right shade of blue and brought the hammer down with a shattering blow. There were enough red chips left from a previous project; she could make a tile with the Cubs logo to set on the windowsill over her kitchen sink. This could be the year.

'Tis a Puzzle

Linda got up from the kitchen table and took her cereal bowl to the sink to rinse it before putting it in the dishwasher. She glanced over at Russell, still in his pajamas and hunched over his granola, attacking the *Star's* crossword puzzle with his ballpoint pen. It was Monday—this was fast and furious action. Later in the week, when the puzzles grew in difficulty, the pace would slow. Scribbles would be interspersed with chewing of the pen. Russell took seriously the admonition to exercise his brain in retirement.

Linda still worked; she had another seven months at Meridian Bank before she would be fully vested for retirement. She glanced at the clock on the microwave and reached for the jacket to her navy pantsuit, and her handbag, both hanging on a spare chair at the table.

"See you later, then," she didn't want to interrupt, but didn't want to leave without serving notice to her husband that she was out the door.

"Okay." Russell glanced up mid-scribble. "Later."

As Linda backed her car out of the drive she tried to remember the last time her husband had kissed her goodbye. He used to give her a quick peck every morning when he left for work at the Chrysler plant—in those days he left the house before she did. Maybe the person leaving was supposed to instigate the kiss goodbye—and so it was her "fault" if she didn't get a goodbye smooch now. But it could be dangerous to try to stick your face between Russell and the *Star* crossword—you could get stabbed with a ballpoint pen. It seemed easier to just leave; easier, but somehow lacking.

She was so absorbed in thought she had to stomp on the brake when she suddenly saw Fred, from two houses down, barreling down the sidewalk in his tracksuit.

That was close! She needed to be less distracted. But what about Fred? Couldn't *he* slow down a little and wait for *her*—a woman on her way to work—to back out of the drive? Nope. Fred was another retiree—this one diligently tending to his exercise regime.

Whatever happened to sitting on the porch with a good book? Linda recalled the fantasies she had had of the retirement she would share with Russell. Walks along the bikepath on pretty autumn mornings. Afternoon movies at special senior rates. There were crossword puzzles involved—but they worked them together, combining their various interests to come up with the answers. That bubble had been burst early on in Russell's retirement.

"You're an old farm girl," he had teased, "what's a four letter word for farm wagon that begins with a 'w' and ends with an 'n'?"

"First of all—I'm not an old farm girl. I spent a few summers on my grandmother's farm, that's all. And second, I haven't a clue what that word would be. Four letters?"

So, in the blink of an eye, she had been tested and come up wanting. She was useless. Only on very rare occasions did Russell bother asking for her help—when he thought it was something she should know.

"You know all about flowers; what's the state flower of Alabama?"

Linda liked her job. She looked forward to going to work every day—well, most days. Sometimes she stood in front of the closet too long, trying to decide what to wear. It'd be nice not to have to make that decision every day—nice not to have to make sure there was something presentable—and clean—available. Linda's sister, Therese, took early retirement last year when the phone company made her an offer she couldn't refuse. There were days when Therese barely got out of her pajamas—sometimes didn't even take a shower. *And she bragged about it!* Linda and Therese were not a whole lot alike; it's funny how that can happen with people who supposedly have the same genetic makeup.

So Linda did not envision spending a whole lot of time hanging out with her sister when she was retired. She had good friends at work—Celia and Rosemary. The three of them had worked together for a long time. Linda was somewhat older, Celia and Rosemary weren't quite ready to retire. It would be a few years before they'd be available to go for coffee or do lunch or take a day trip somewhere.

"Hey there, Linda." The young security guard was sharp—he had made it his business to learn everybody's name within just a few days of being hired. So even though she kept her nametag in her desk, Rob was able to greet her by name every morning.

"Hey yourself, Rob. Everything under control?"

"It is now that you're here," he responded.

"Got that right." She hadn't bothered to check to see if he greeted everybody the same way—but Linda thought it was possible. Nevertheless, she appreciated his playful recognition of her status as one of the vice presidents of the bank—someone who did, indeed, have more than a little responsibility for keeping everything under control. She'd worked hard, put in her time, and had been promoted to vice president eight years ago.

"Probably needed to make sure they had enough females at the top," had been Russell's comment when she burst through the door that night after work with her surprise announcement. Linda had her own suspicions along that line but thought it less than chivalrous of her husband to make such an observation. But that was Russell for you. Or, maybe there was something about her promotion that rankled him a little. He had worked on the production floor at Chrysler forever—made good money, a lot more than Linda ever dreamed of making even with this promotion—but he didn't go to work in a suit and tie. Maybe she was just imagining a tiny bit of resentment. "The Suits" at Chrysler were a pain in the neck as far as Russell was concerned.

"Fred wants to see you," Bonnie told her as she passed her assistant's desk on the way to her office.

The president of the bank prided himself on being the first one in the office every day, so Linda wasn't concerned about his being here ahead of her.

"Have a chair. You want some coffee?" Fred asked as she came in. He rose and closed the door.

Uh-oh.

"I felt we should touch base on your future plans," Fred said.

"Okay…" Linda wasn't sure what he meant exactly.

"I mean, I know you've previously spoken about retiring as soon as you were eligible for full benefits. And that's coming up soon, isn't it?"

"Right."

"Do you have big plans for your retirement? Places to go? People to see?"

"Not really." Linda was uncomfortable admitting this.

"And, if I remember correctly, your husband is already retired?"

"Yes. He's been retired for a little over a year."

"So I thought maybe you had plans made for when both of you are retired. Travel plans? A move to a warmer climate?"

"No." Linda crossed and uncrossed her ankles. "Russell kind of likes being at home...not doing anything special."

"How about you?" Fred smiled to show this was a friendly question, not an inquisition about her marriage.

"Oh, I'm good with that."

"Are you happy in your work?"

"Oh, yes!"

"You seem to be," Fred said. He got up from behind his desk and came around to sit in the chair beside her, moving it a little so he was more or less facing her rather than sitting alongside. "And we've been very happy with your work."

"Good." Linda wondered if this was standard exit-interview jargon.

"In fact, we really hate to see you leave," Fred said.

"I'm actually dreading the day myself," Linda admitted, feeling herself exhale a breath she didn't realize she'd been holding.

"Well, then, maybe you'd consider staying on?"

"Really?!" Linda sat taller, her spine straightening at this unexpected suggestion.

"Really. We'll be hiring a few new people in the next few months, and I think you'd be the ideal person to train them, bring them up to speed. Your work ethic has always been exemplary—I would hope you'd be able to pass that on to any new staff."

Linda sat in stunned silence.

"If that appeals to you?" Fred hastened to ask. "I wouldn't want to upset your applecart at home."

Linda shook her head yes, than no.

"We won't add to your workload. We'd pass some of your present duties on to others—mostly to Jeffrey, he's in line for a vice-presidency within the next year or so."

"Right…" she wished she could summon an intelligent response.

"And we'd be willing to sweeten the deal by giving you a ten percent raise."

Linda's eyes widened.

"Couldn't expect you to delay your retirement without some reward, could we?" Fred smiled at her again. She knew she should say something…anything. "Why don't you think about it for a few days—talk it over with your husband—and then let me know if you're willing to stay on with us a little longer."

"How much longer?" Linda immediately regretted her question, because she didn't really care, but she was curious.

"Oh, I think at least a year or two, if that's alright with you. We can play it by ear."

She kind of nodded again. Fred stood, signaling the end of their conversation. Linda got to her feet, shook Fred's hand, and managed to find her way out. When she got to her own office, her assistant looked up, frankly inquisitive. Linda brushed quickly by Bonnie's desk, went in, closed the door, sat at her desk, and burst into tears.

Russell was watching golf on TV when Linda arrived home from work that evening. Sapphire, the cat they had inherited when their daughter moved to an apartment that didn't allow pets, was curled up in his lap. Russell didn't play golf, but Linda hoped that adding the Golf Channel to their cable package would inspire him. It hadn't worked so far, but they'd only had the channel for a month. Russell seemed to be getting lumpier day by day, maybe she needed to push the golf thing a little.

"Oh, that looks nice," Linda said. "Where are they playing?" She set her purse down and gave Russell a bit of a kiss on the cheek before easing herself out of her jacket.

"California," he said, carefully following a Rory McIlroy putt as it rolled slowly but surely across the green and into the cup. He gave a fist pump then looked at her with a big grin—"Luck of the Irish!"

"Speaking of luck…" Linda began, intending to launch into the little speech she had rehearsed off and on for much of the afternoon.

"Wait just a sec—Tiger's about to tee off." Russell held up his hand to ward off any further conversation.

Linda sighed and went to change her clothes before starting dinner. Well, the part about getting him interested in golf had worked—but getting him out of the house to actually play golf himself would be another matter. She carefully hung her pantsuit in her closet, then eased into her jeans and Cubs shirt. Linda felt herself relax a notch just putting on the blue jeans and t-shirt. There was definitely a physical comfort to wearing cotton—a tactile thing that she had begun to recognize and appreciate only in the last few years. If she were retired, she could wear jeans all day most days.

Linda had to pass through the living room again to get to the kitchen. Russell glanced up as she went by. "Tiger's not having a very good day," he reported, standing and clicking the OFF button on the remote. Sapphire tumbled softly to the carpet, then performed a long end-of-nap stretch.

"Why don't you fix us a drink?" Linda suggested, as Russell and Sapphire followed her into the kitchen.

"Good idea—you want gin or vodka?"

"Vodka, I think." She opened the refrigerator and handed him a lime and grabbed the chicken breasts she was going to pan-sauté for supper, then ducked out of the way as Russell opened the freezer to retrieve the chilled bottle of Ketel One.

"Maybe I should take up golf," Russell suggested as he dropped ice cubes into two tall glasses.

"That sounds like a good idea," Linda struggled to keep her response low-key.

"I'm probably too old, though. And what would Sapphire do with me gone for hours at a time?" Russell poured a little vodka in her glass, a little more in his, then added lots of diet tonic to both.

"She managed just fine when we were both working," Linda pointed out.

"She did, didn't she? And you'll be retiring soon, so she'll have you around for company." Russell handed her a glass and then clinked his to hers. "Are we drinking to something special?"

"To golf…" Linda suggested.

"To retirement," Russell replied.

Linda turned away and took a sip of her drink, holding the icy cold liquid in her mouth, inhaling the tang of the lime, savoring the smooth taste of the vodka. For just a moment, she closed her eyes and was elsewhere. She could understand why some women became drunks in their old age.

When she opened her eyes, Russell was looking at her. "Everything all right?"

"Fine." It was funny how he could be so unaware of some of her frustrations some of the time, but other times his radar seemed to be acutely tuned in.

"Want me to set the table?" he asked.

"Sure." Did he need permission? Oh, now she *was* getting persnickety. The dear man was just trying to be helpful—and she's finding something wrong with that? Linda took another gulp of her drink and set the glass down. She rolled a lemon around on the cutting board and got out her zester, one of her favorite kitchen instruments. All it took was a couple of swipes and the air was filled with the incomparable fresh smell of lemon. A little pile of lemon zest appeared, ready to put some zip into whatever you were making—in this case, a Dijon marinade for the chicken breasts. Linda liked to cook. She would enjoy having more time to experiment with new recipes—whenever she retired.

While the chicken was browning, Linda chopped carrots and tomatoes, peeled and sliced part of a cucumber, and rinsed the salad greens. She turned the chicken breasts over, poured the remaining marinade over them, then put a lid on the pan to let them cook a little longer.

Russell had wandered out into the backyard after he set the table, Linda found him sitting in one of the deck chairs on the patio, eyes closed and head bobbing forward on his chest.

"About that retirement thing," she began.

Russell's eyes flew open and he grinned sheepishly at her. "I was all worn out from setting the table," he said.

"Right." Linda settled in the chair next to his, fixed her eyes on him, and gave Russell a tentative smile.

"Do I need to fix myself another drink?" he asked, draining his glass.

"No, don't do that." Linda put her hand on top of his—she didn't want him to get up. Not now. "We have to talk about *my* retirement."

"What's to talk about? You wanna make plans? Take a trip somewhere?"

"No, that's just it," Linda took her hand away and used both of them to hold onto her drink. "They've asked me to stay on at the bank." There, she'd said it.

"Stay on? What for? How long?"

"Fred thinks I would be good at helping train some of the new staffers we'll be hiring in the next several months."

"Several months?"

"In fact, he'd actually like me to stay on for as long as a couple more years."

"But you were all set to retire. Right? In just six or seven months? That's not fair, is it?"

"Actually, I'd *like* to stay on, Russ."

"C'mon. Are you serious?" Russell stood and looked at her. "I mean, you've put in your time. You deserve to take it easy."

"I'm not so sure I'm ready to 'take it easy.'" Linda remained seated, hoping Russell would sit back down. "I like my job. And it's not like we've made any special plans."

"Well, we could."

"The extra money I'll be earning could help pay for some of those plans."

"But what am I supposed to do?"

"Just what you've been doing. You've been happy these last few months, haven't you? With your crossword puzzles...and now you're going to take up golf."

"That's not for sure." Russell remained standing, kind of shifting from one foot to the other.

"Well, it's a possibility."

"I need another drink," he said, and abruptly turned to go back in the house.

Dinner was a quiet affair…until Russell turned on the TV. "I just want to see how that tournament turned out." What he obviously did not want to do was discuss Linda's non-retirement. The avoidance lasted throughout the evening.

"Are you coming to bed soon?" Linda asked as she bent to give him a goodnight kiss.

"I'm not very tired." This, from the same man whose head had been nap-bobbing on the patio just a few hours earlier.

And so Linda went to work the next day with nothing really resolved. Fred poked his head in the door of her office. "Did you and your hubby have a chance to talk things over?"

"Not really. We were both kind of busy last night. We'll probably have more time over the weekend."

"Good." He paused. "Do you think there's going to be a problem with you staying on?"

"Oh, no." She summoned a reassuring smile. "I just need to find the right time to bring it up."

"Okay. I'll check in with you Monday." He gave the door-frame a little pat. "Have a good weekend."

"Right. You, too."

Why didn't she just tell Fred she'd be staying on? She was going to—she knew that. Even if Russell raised a fuss. Did she really need his permission? Maybe not his *permission*—but at least his agreement would be nice. Linda was not looking forward to the weekend.

She spent Saturday tiptoeing around on the proverbial eggshells while Russell was in the house. Thankfully, he was inventing all kinds of reasons not to be around—off to the hardware store and the library, both places where he could spend an inordinate amount of time. And Saturday night they were more or less forced to avoid the subject when they went to dinner with their friends, Barry and Sue. Linda realized she was the only one in the foursome who was not retired, even though Sue was a few years younger. They yakked on and on about the cruise they had just enjoyed.

"We had so much fun we're already making plans for our next one. One of those river cruises in Europe, I think," Sue proclaimed.

"What's wrong with this country?" Russell asked.

"Nothing, nothing. But we've seen pretty much all there is to see here," Barry hastened to point out.

"All there is to see?" Russell's challenge was aborted by the waiter coming to ask if they wanted dessert.

And then Russell and Linda were home—just the two of them. Russell walked straight to his recliner and was reaching for the remote when Linda stopped him.

"We can't avoid this discussion any longer, Russ."

"What discussion?"

"You know…about the offer the bank made me…to stay on."

"I just don't see why you don't want to retire," Russell began. "We could travel like Barry and Sue."

"If we could agree on where we wanted to go."

"We'd figure it out."

"But the places we want to go see will still be there if we wait a couple more years." Linda thought this would sound logical, even to Russell.

"*They* might be, but will we?" Russell plunked into his recliner.

"What are you saying?"

"I'm just saying, you never know when one of us is going to…you know… kick off."

"Is there something you're not telling me?" Linda asked. "I thought you got a clean bill of health from the doctor just a couple of months ago."

"So? That doesn't mean something won't happen…or some terrible disease won't strike…in the next couple years. Or next month." Russell pointed the remote at her for emphasis.

"Something could 'happen' next week, Russ. We can't go around making decisions on something *maybe* happening."

"But it might." Russell clicked the TV on, and turned away. Then he clicked it off again. "What about that trip we talked about—taking Heidi's kids to D.C.?" Again with the remote pointed at her.

"What about it?"

"Those kids are gonna be teenagers and not wanting to go anywhere with their doddering old grandparents by the time you're ready to retire and spend a little time with the rest of us."

Linda was dumbfounded. "You're not making any sense."

"Gotcha on that one, didn't I?"

"I'm going to make myself a drink." Linda needed to hit the pause button on this conversation.

"Bring me a beer while you're at it, will ya?"

There it was—a perfect example of what her days and nights of retirement would be like. Russell in his recliner with the all-powerful remote, and Linda waiting on him hand and foot. She opened the refrigerator door and surveyed its contents, then made a managerial decision.

Linda came back into the living room with two small glasses of tomato juice.

"What's this? We can't be out of beer?"

"I just think that if we're going to have a reasonable discussion, neither one of us needs any more alcohol."

"I can be reasonable and drink beer at the same time." Russell grinned at her, then reached up to click his juice glass against hers. "Truce?"

"Truce." Linda sat down on the ottoman.

"I just wish you could understand that this offer means a lot to me. I'm flattered, sure—but it's also like a validation of the work I've been doing—work I like doing."

"More than you like bringing me beers?" he teased.

"I know that's hard to believe…" she realized Russell understood more than she thought he did.

"How about this?" Linda set her glass down on the end table and leaned forward with her hands clasped in front of her. "How about if I tell Fred I'll stay another year? Twelve months. Then I'll retire for sure."

"Why will you be ready then, but you're not now?"

"At least I will have taken advantage of this opportunity. I won't have regrets about having turned down what I think is a very appealing offer." She paused. "And in the meantime, you can get on the computer and plan a trip for us with the grandkids. And maybe one for just the two of us."

"You're good at this, y'know? This negotiating stuff." Russell picked up one of her hands and brought it to his lips. "I think we've got ourselves a deal."

Linda awoke early the next morning. Something in her subconscious told her she was alone in bed. Sure enough— when she opened one eye to peek over at Russell's side of the bed, it was empty. Didn't even seem to have been slept in.

She got up and went to the open doorway of their bedroom and could hear the TV. He must have fallen asleep watching Saturday Night Live. Linda thought about going back to bed—it was Sunday morning, after all—but knew she wouldn't go back to sleep. Maybe she'd go down and start the coffee before she showered.

One of those half-hours of paid commercial time selling the perfect piece of exercise equipment was quietly attempting to persuade Russell, who appeared to be paying no attention and in a sound sleep in his recliner with his back to her. Should she wake him? She came up behind him; stepped closer.

Something was wrong. There was a sour odor. She reached over to shake his shoulder but stopped. Ohmigod. Something was terribly wrong. She did then—she put her hand on his shoulder at the same time she stepped around for a better look.

"Russell? Russell!" He was grey, his mouth hung open, his pants were soiled. She picked up the remote that had fallen to the floor and put it on the end table next to him. She shook his knee. "Russell!"

Call 9-1-1. There might still be time. She stumbled to the kitchen and punched in the numbers.

Ten days later, Linda was back in the office. "Take as much time as you want," had been Fred's admonition. And she had. After the days of funeral arranging and dazed family gathering and trying to sort out who would sleep where—they had all gone back to their respective homes.

"Come with us for a week or so," Adriana—her sweet daughter-in-law had urged.

"No, maybe I'll come for a visit later." She didn't want to be the one who had to explain to Benjamin and Marcy why their grandfather was not with her. Linda wasn't sure *she* knew why Russell wasn't still around to play "Go Fish" with them.

At least here in the office, there was some semblance of routine. No question what to do next. Her duties were known to her and she busied herself right through lunch and on up to five o'clock.

"Are you sure you're all right?" Rosemary asked as she peeked her head in the door of Linda's office.

Linda nodded.

"You want to go have a drink?" Rosemary half-heartedly suggested.

"No." They both knew that wasn't going to be a good path to go down. "I'll be okay, honest. I just want to finish up with this." Linda pointed at her computer screen as if there was an all-consuming project to be completed.

"Okay, then. See you tomorrow."

"Right."

Linda at last forced herself to go home. She opened the front door to overwhelming silence. Linda walked over to Russell's recliner, lightly caressed the cool leather surface of the arm and, after a moment of hesitation, she sat down in the chair. Sapphire appeared out of nowhere and jumped into her lap.

"Now what do we do?" she asked the cat.

Cherry Jam

Tall, thin, and fond of her gin, Florence felt pretty smug about reaching her seventy-fifth birthday with—as her internist proclaimed—"the heart rate and blood pressure of a woman half your age!" She suspected it had less to do with lifestyle than with genes—her great-grandmother, after whom she was named, had lived to be ninety-three.

Florence also credited her easy laissez-faire. "Don't get your undies in a bundle" had been her late husband's attitude, and although he died of a heart attack on the eve of his sixty-second birthday, she thought those were good words to live by.

She had been a flower child in the Sixties, and was proud to claim the "liberal" label. It made no difference to her if the two gentlemen who lived next door shared a bed, or if the boy she once dated in high school was now a she, "Renee," and a competent cosmetologist. No worries.

She created her own little oasis of serenity in a world that, on some days, seemed to be going to hell in a handbasket.

There was one pet peeve that irritated Florence—when somebody presumed to call her "Flo."

"Florence," she'd correct whomever.

Sometimes the person who had stepped over the line understood. Sometimes they were clueless.

"My mother named me Florence, after my great-grand-mother," she pointed out, when a second violation occurred.

Operating on three-strikes-and-you're-out, the final plea was delivered with her hand resting meaningfully on the offender's arm, "Please, 'Florence'." After that, she just gave up. Some people simply cannot be educated.

Better to turn one's attention elsewhere. She liked sitting on her patio with her new "*Peterson Field Guide to Birds of North Central America*" in her lap and her gin-and-tonic in hand. She purchased a very nice birdbath which attracted a steady flow of customers just at cocktail hour. The house finches—the male with his pretty rosy head and chest, and the less ostentatious female—came in pairs. Almost invariably, one would light at the rim of the birdbath, followed by the other, to sip and join her in the late afternoon. Life was good.

Florence's patio was out her kitchen door and bridged the gap between house and garage. The branches of a cherry tree hung over a corner of the patio, with pretty pink-tinged papery blossoms in the spring, and bird-attracting plump cherries in summer. Also, a bit of a mess in that corner, but easily cleaned up with a broom and soapy water. She certainly didn't want to prune back the tree.

On this July afternoon, the cherries were beginning to ripen. Also, her drink was beginning to disappear. Florence went back inside to add more ice to her glass, a little gin, and a generous pour of tonic—she always made her second drink on the weak side. Being in the kitchen made her wonder what she would have for her dinner. She glanced around as if something might pop up ready-made. Out the window, some movement on the patio caught the corner of her eye. She leaned in to get a better look.

Someone was on her patio. Not anyone she knew. This was a large black male—large in the sense that he was bulky, not really tall. Where had he come from? More importantly, what was he doing on her patio?

Florence looked around for a weapon. The broom she used to sweep off the patio was right by the back door. Was she going to "shoo" this person away? She moved off to the side of the window so she could watch the interloper without being seen.

He was picking *her* cherries. He hurriedly picked a bunch—as many as he could hold in his hands—then glanced toward the kitchen door and made for the alley behind her garage.

Florence exhaled. Relaxed the grip on her broom. Had she really thought he would come in the house? Attack her? She sat down on the closest kitchen chair and took a gulp of her gin. It was too early to conclude her patio cocktail hour but Florence wasn't sure she felt—what was the word?—comfortable, about returning to her sacred space. Her favorite spot in all the world now felt threatened. Intruded upon.

She stood and looked out the window again. A breeze rippled the leaves of the cherry tree, creating a movement of shadow across the patio that seemed inviting an hour ago, but now appeared sinister.

Florence turned away, dithered about her kitchen for a while, finally scrambled two eggs and ate them with toast and cherry jam at her kitchen table, glancing frequently out the kitchen window. Eventually, she took the crossword puzzle from the morning paper and went to bed, double-checking to be sure both the front and back doors were locked. Maybe tomorrow she would check into getting one of those motion-detector lights installed on the garage.

The next morning Florence was really ticked with herself. First of all, she questioned her integrity as a strong proponent of equal rights for men and women, black and white. Last night she had tangled with the bedsheets, and with the thought that she would not have been as threatened if the man on the patio had been white. Could it be that she was just as guilty of bias as some of the police officers being called on the carpet across the country for their racial profiling?

Second, why on earth would she allow anybody—black, green, white, or whatever color—to rob her of her place on the patio? Her hand almost shook as she poured her first cup of coffee and marched out the back door to reclaim her spot on the chaise under the cherry tree.

Florence didn't calm down and relax until she was on her second cup. Then, as Mr. and Mrs. House Finch paused to sip from the birdbath, Florence took a deep breath and forced herself to look around and appreciate the tranquil morning. The cherries were pretty much all red now, very few were still yellow. She should move the chaise out from under the tree or it would be a mess when the cherries started dropping.

Why would someone want her cherries?

Probably because he was hungry, dummy.

Florence sat up abruptly, erect now in realization. Perhaps he was just picking cherries because he could; or perhaps he was picking cherries because that was all he had to eat yesterday. If that was the case, he was likely to have a bit of a stomach ache. Maybe he already had a stomach ache—or hunger pangs—when he happened upon her cherry tree.

Florence marched back in the house, made a peanut butter and cherry jam sandwich on healthy whole wheat bread, put it on a paper plate and covered it with plastic wrap, then set it on the little table next to the chaise.

She was tempted to hang around in the kitchen and watch to see if he would come back—and if he did, if he would take the sandwich. But Florence forced herself to carry on with her normal routine, which meant she was off to the grocery store. More whole wheat bread, maybe some cold cuts and cheese, those little individual yogurts, a few apples, and another bottle of gin.

When she got back home, she almost ran into the side of her garage craning her neck from the car to see if the sandwich was gone. It was. Gone.

Later, when Florence took her garbage out, she spotted the paper plate and plastic wrap in the garbage can.

So, the next morning, Florence made a ham and cheese sandwich and put it on a paper plate. She added some of those little baby carrots and decided it looked very healthy indeed.

This time, she didn't have to go to the grocery store, but she couldn't very well spend her whole day hanging out in the kitchen watching for this hungry man. She had laundry to do.

Florence was just coming up the basement stairs when she heard a tentative knock at her back door. There he was—the hungry man. The sun was in back of him, his face was in shadow. So she was taken aback when she opened the door a bit and saw that he was quite young—just a boy.

"Yes?" she said. She didn't know what else to say. She kept the opening narrow.

"Do you need your grass cut or something?" he asked.

Florence opened the door a little wider in surprise. "My grass cut? Does it need it?"

"It's just...I would like to pay you for the sandwiches, but I don't have any money."

She studied him carefully. "What's your name?"

"Barry."

"How do you do? I'm Florence...Mrs. Lowell." She extended her hand in a greeting that felt ridiculously formal. "How old are you?"

"I'll be fourteen next week."

"Do you know how to run a lawnmower?"

"Not really, but I could learn."

"And I could probably teach you." Florence stepped out the door onto the patio. He was not quite as tall as she. "But I don't think the lawn needs mowing. I just did it a couple of days ago." They scrutinized her small backyard.

"Let's sit a minute," she suggested, and plopped into one of the two aluminum chairs, choosing the more rickety one and hoping the other would hold Barry. The plate that had held the sandwich was empty.

"Are you thirsty? Would you like a glass of water?"

Barry nodded. "Yes. Yes, please."

"Wait here," she said, when the boy looked uncertain about whether he should follow her into the house.

When Florence returned with water for each of them, he was gone. She took a few steps onto the patio to peer closely at the cherry tree, as if the boy may have disappeared up amongst its branches. She went to look in the garage window, then down the alley. Gone. He must have run to be out of sight so quickly.

Florence put her glass down on the table and then dumped the water from the boy's glass onto a nearby geranium and took the glass inside. She stopped to look in the little mirror she had hung just inside the door—the perfect place to put on lipstick on her way out, if she was feeling that fussy. Surveying her countenance, she decided her shorn grey curls could stand brushing but she didn't look that scary. Maybe she looked like a mean teacher Barry once had in school?

She went down to the basement to transfer her laundry from the washer to the dryer, then went back out to the patio to drink her glass of water. Alone.

The next morning, Florence made another ham and cheese sandwich, arranged it on a paper plate with baby carrots, and put it out on the patio. She added a little note: *I have a job for you.*

So she wasn't surprised when, a little while later, she heard a knock on her back door.

"You have a job?" Barry asked, holding up the note as evidence.

"I do. How do you feel about getting up on a ladder?"

"I can do that," he assured her.

"Well, I know you're good at picking the cherries off the lower branches, but let's see how good you are at getting those cherries that are out of reach."

He lowered his eyes and looked away.

"I'm just teasing. Sorry. C'mon, help me get the ladder out of the garage." Florence realized she would have to tread lightly.

She also discovered it was a lot easier to carry the ladder when you had someone to grab the other end. They set it up in the grass under the far reaches of the tree.

"Oops! I didn't realize you hadn't eaten yet," Florence said when she saw the sandwich still on the paper plate. "Why don't you go ahead and eat? I'll get a bucket for the cherries."

"Okay." Barry sat down in one of the aluminum chairs and had the sandwich half gone by the time she was in her back door.

She rinsed out a scrub bucket and brought it to the patio, along with a glass of water for Barry. She had to bite her tongue to keep from saying something like *I hope this glass of water doesn't make you run away again.*

But he didn't run. Instead, he took a couple deep gulps of water, then, still carrying the glass, followed her over to where she stood beside the ladder.

"Now, Barry, I need you to be very careful. Please don't fall off the ladder and break your neck."

"I won't." He was very serious. She really had to soft-pedal her teasing.

"There's way more cherries on this tree than we'll need, so just pick those that are easy for you to reach. Then move the ladder to another part of the tree and pick the easy ones there."

"Okay." Barry looked as if he wasn't quite sure about something.

"Any questions?"

"Are we just going to eat all these cherries? Or are you going to make pie?"

"Jam. I'm going to make jam."

"Oh."

"Maybe you could help me."

"Really?"

"Really. But first we need cherries." She handed him the bucket and Barry went up the ladder a couple of steps. He paused, then went up a couple more. "That's high enough. Don't go any higher, okay?"

"Okay." He seemed to agree—four steps up was high enough.

She was all the way inside before she stuck her head out the door with a pertinent afterthought.

"And just pick the really red ones. You can come back and pick the others when they get ripe."

"Okay."

After he had been picking cherries for almost an hour, Florence went out to check on him. She saw that he had moved the ladder at least once, and that the bucket was almost brimful.

"Gosh! You're a fast picker!"

He smiled. "The bucket's almost full."

"I see that. Why don't you come on down and rest a bit? I'll get you another glass of water."

He backed down the ladder, carefully carrying the bucket of cherries. "It's heavy," he said, seeming surprised.

"Yes, well, that's a lot of cherries. Set the bucket in the garage where it's cooler. We'll leave it overnight, then make the jam tomorrow."

"Let's sit in the shade," she said, moving one of the aluminum chairs out of the sun and into the shadow cast by the garage. Barry followed suit.

"Have you ever pitted cherries?" Florence asked.

"Nope."

"You have to pit cherries to make pie or jam. You could make jelly without pitting them and just cook 'em up, then run the juice through a sieve, but I like jam better."

Barry had no response to that.

"Pitting cherries is a messy job, and it takes a long time. Even if you're experienced."

He took a drink of water.

"I like these glasses," he said. Florence had filled her two plastic thermal glasses with ice and water. They had the Cubs logo on them.

"You a baseball fan?"

"Hm-hmm."

"The Cubs are doing pretty well this year."

"The Cardinals are doing better."

"You're a Cardinal fan?"

"Yep." He grinned.

"How'd you get to be a Cardinal fan? Are you from St. Louis?"

"My grandpa was from down there, from East St. Louis."

"Ah."

A robin chirped from the cherry tree.

"He doesn't live there anymore?"

"Nope." Barry stood, drained his glass and handed it to her. Apparently this conversation was ended.

Florence got to her feet. "If you'll come by early in the morning, I'll make us some breakfast before we get started on the jam. Do you like pancakes?"

He grinned as if she had asked the silliest question in the world.

"Try to be here by about eight. But don't worry if you're a little late, I won't actually start making pancakes until you get here."

"Okay," he said, and then turned and sauntered off down the alley.

As Florence sipped her gin and tonic on the patio that afternoon, she wondered where the boy went off to. Did he live nearby? Was there no one to feed him? No food in the house?

That night Florence loaded up the dishwasher with canning jars and lids so they'd be all ready for the next day's jam-making. She didn't use the dishwasher all that often anymore; it seemed a waste to run it for just one or two plates, a few pieces of silverware, her coffee cup and her Cubs glass. She usually washed them out in the sink and left them to drain overnight. This night, though, they fit in among the canning jars for a sanitizing wash.

In bed, she found it difficult to concentrate on the crossword puzzle. Her thoughts wandered to the next day's jam-making and to her newfound helper.

The next morning was rainy and gray, a good day to be inside. Jam-making could stain your clothes, so she pulled on her painting jeans and denim shirt. Before she unloaded the dishwasher, Florence made the pancake batter so it could rest a bit before being spooned into the skillet. Would Barry show up if he had to walk through the rain to get here? When she heard a knock at her back door, she glanced at the clock—7:55.

"Come in!" she called, and grinned at Barry when he entered her kitchen. His t-shirt was soaked and he stood just inside the door, hesitating.

"Come in, come in," Florence urged.

"My shoes are all squishy."

"Oh. Well, just take them off. Leave them on the doormat. Don't worry, my kitchen floor won't get hurt by a few raindrops. And, we're going to be making a lot bigger mess in here anyway."

He easily shed his untied sneakers.

"Wait here a minute," she said, leaving the kitchen and returning a moment later with a clean dry t-shirt, XL, with a Cubs logo.

"Sorry, I don't have any Cardinal shirts. This is an old one of my husband's. See? It's from the 1998 Spring Training camp."

"This shirt's older than me," observed Barry, holding it out in front of him. He continued to study the shirt until Florence realized he did not want to change in front of her.

"There's a bathroom over there by the basement stairs," she pointed, and moved to the stove to fire up the burner under the skillet.

After they shared a mountain of pancakes and a couple cups of coffee, Florence loaded their breakfast dishes into the dishwasher and looked out the window. "It's only sprinkling at the moment. It'd be a good time for you to go out and get the bucket of cherries."

Barry elected to go barefoot rather than get back into his squishy shoes, then shuffled about on the doormat to dry his feet before bringing the bucket of bright red cherries over to Florence at the sink.

She dumped the bucket of cherries in the sink to wash them, then divided the whole lot into a couple of big bowls. She spread brown paper grocery bags on the kitchen table and plunked the empty Dutch oven between them.

"If we were going in the jam-making business, I'd invest in a cherry pitter," Florence explained. "But I've found using a paper clip is pretty efficient."

She showed Barry how to open up the paper clip and slide it into the cherry to pull out the pit. He got the hang of it right away.

They launched into the bowls of cherries. It was, as she had warned him, messy work. Cherry juice was soon dribbling down their arms.

"We'll have to use lots of sugar to make jam with these cherries," Florence remarked. "They're kind of sour."

"Hm-hmm." Barry nodded.

"I read a poem once that said that soldiers on their way to battle at Gettysburg ate cherries off the tree. During the Civil War."

"Too bad they didn't have pie—or jam." Barry empathized.

"Some kinds of cherries are sweet right off the tree, but these *are* pretty sour. Did you get a stomach ache from eating them?"

"My stomach wasn't doing too good anyhow."

"You must have been pretty hungry to be eating these cherries right off the tree."

"Yeah."

"So, isn't there anything to eat at your house?"

"Not really."

"How come?"

Barry was silent, studiously working at pitting the cherry in hand.

"Do you live with your mom? Your grandmother?"

"My mom."

"So she's hungry, too?"

"She's in jail, so I think she gets to eat there."

"Your mom's in jail?"

He nodded almost imperceptibly and reached for another cherry without looking at Florence. She studied him, trying to decide what to ask next, if anything. She got up from the table and filled the Cubs glasses with ice and water. Back at the table, she could hear the kitchen wall clock ticking as a silence hung in the air.

"Do you want to tell me why your mom is in jail?"

He kept his head down. "Sometimes when she goes off her meds she does crazy stuff." He looked up at Florence. "She was trying to shoplift some chicken from the Wal-Mart but she got caught." He shrugged. His tone was so matter-of-fact it nearly broke Florence's heart.

"Do you know how long she'll be there?"

He shook his head. "She doesn't have bail money, and sometimes it takes a long time before you even see the judge."

"So this has happened before?"

"Yeah." The kitchen darkened as it began to rain again in earnest.

"Oh, Barry."

"But not a lot," he assured her. "And this time it's not so bad. Last time I got sent to live with my grandma in Joliet. I had to stay with her even after my mom got out of jail, until they said it was okay for me to live with my mom again."

"Why didn't that happen this time?"

"I think my mom didn't tell about me. No cops or anybody came looking for me."

"Maybe they will when she appears before the judge?"

"Maybe," he agreed. "But if I can make it till my birthday, then it's okay. I can live by myself."

"At fourteen?"

"Yep."

"Are you sure? How do you know this?"

"My friend Celeste told me. Her mom is crazy, too." Again with the shrug of the shoulders.

This was more information than Florence could digest in one sitting. She stood and went over to the sink to refill her water glass. Then she refilled Barry's glass and sat down again at the table. She looked at Barry, his head down, appearing to concentrate on the cherry in hand.

"We're doing really well," she said. "We'll have these cherries cooking in no time." He looked up. "Wait till you taste this jam; you'll want it on your pancakes instead of syrup," she promised.

Barry grinned.

Florence got up again to turn on the kitchen radio, already set at her favorite classical FM station. "I hope you don't mind some music, it'll help us keep a rhythm going." They had the cherries, pectin and sugar cooking on top of the stove before lunchtime. Florence spooned some onto saltines so they could each have a taste.

"What do you think?" she asked, as Barry bit into his.

He gave her a thumbs up.

"Didn't I tell you?" She started ladling jam into jars, then wiping their rims. "Here," she handed him a jar. "You can put the lids on. That flat piece first, then the round band."

Florence wished she had a reason to keep Barry there for the rest of the day, but she knew that wasn't going to work. He didn't mind helping to make cherry jam, but he wasn't going to spend the rest of his day answering her many questions. He probably already regretted telling her as much as he had.

"These jars have to go into a water bath, cook a bit and then cool, so I can't give you one to take home now. But come by tomorrow and I'll give you some."

"Okay." He was standing at her back door, his hand on the knob. "What about this shirt?"

"Oh, you can keep that. Unless you don't want to be seen in a Cub shirt?"

"It's alright, I'll wear it at night when it's dark out."

She laughed. "How about coming by about noon tomorrow for your jar of jam? I might even give you two, since you did so much of the work."

"It's a deal." And he was gone.

Noon meant she'd be able to give him lunch.

And thus was created what Florence would forever after think of as "The Summer of Barry." She checked with a social worker friend and found that his information was correct. "Probably the best thing you can do is just be his friend, feed him regularly, and hope that keeps him out of trouble," her friend advised.

"Trouble" was something she worried about. Florence thought about asking Barry to move in with her—just temporarily—but decided that wouldn't help him or his mom in the long run. Barry was learning to be self-reliant, a quality that would be a big help as the two of them worked their way through this particular trouble.

So she spent the summer thinking of chores for him to do and cooking for two again. When school started, he told her he wouldn't be able to come by as often, but he'd check in with her on weekends. She knew he could get lunch at school, maybe even breakfast.

One Saturday in early October, he told her his mom was home again and was in some program the court had set up for her.

Florence gave him a hug; she figured he wouldn't stop by as often now that he had his mother to look after.

"You know you can always come by if there's a problem, if you need some help," she told him.

He nodded, then strode down the alley away from her. He turned at the end of the alley and gave her a thumbs up. As she turned to go in the house, yellowing leaves swirled from the cherry tree to the patio. Tomorrow, she'd have to put the chaise in the garage.

Credits

"Garage Sale" originally appeared in *Slippery Elm*; "Should the Dish Run Away with the Spoon?" in *Hypertext*; "A Not-So-Fond Farewell" in *The Raven's Perch*; "Kuzhi" and "Cherry Jam" (as "Paper Plates") in *Kippis!*; "Who's in Charge Here, Anyway?" in *The Oasis Journal*; "To Lego or Not" in *Adanna Literary Journal*; "Pickiing Up the Pieces" in *Two Cities Review*; and "'Tis a Puzzle" in *Adelaide Literary Journal*.

Acknowledgements

These stories would not exist if it were not for the writing groups in Tucson and Galena who have critiqued and applauded my work all along the way—providing impetus to write and encouragement to keep at it. I owe special thanks to Roslyn Schiffman for her assistance with "Kuzhi," to Barbara Sattler for her continued vigilance and shared cups of coffee at Raging Sage. In Rockford, my neighbor Rosaria Mercuri-Ford, just happened to be a teacher of German and of vital assistance in bringing "Ostersonntag" to the printed page—as was Yolanda Weisensel, proprietor of the Camp Grant Museum. Thanks to Linda Goetz for the ceramics lesson needed for "Picking Up the Pieces." Mary Gubbe Lee, MS, assisted me with "Cherry Jam." I am indebted to writer instructor friends Patricia McNair and Christine Maul Rice at the Shake Rag Alley workshops in Mineral Point, Wisconsin, for the inspiration as well as the practical advice they provided. My editor extraordinaire, Gary Houy, helped shape these stories into presentable form and for that I am grateful.

About the Author

Mary Ann Presman's first job was as a "page" in the branch of the local public library—which meant she shelved books. When business was slow, she was actually paid (seventy-cents an hour) while she hid behind bookcases and read to her heart's content. Thus began a lifelong love of reading that blossomed into a fondness for words which served her well in various careers as an advertising copywriter, Congressional press secretary, radio disk jockey, and TV weather person. In retirement, she began to attend writing workshops and was encouraged by the expert guidance and generous friendship of Jim Shepard, Julia Glass and Pam Houston, among others. She has evolved into a writer of short stories and a playwright, fortunately nurtured by two writing groups—one in Tucson founded by Margaret Park, and the other in Galena, Illinois, led by Peggy Stortz. She co-authored a collection of stories with James Wolfe—"Curse? There Ain't No Stinkin' Chicago Cubs Curse," and some of her other stories have appeared in various print and online literary journals as well as in anthologies compiled by the Ex Libris Writers of Galena. Mary Ann and her husband Bob live happily in Rockford, Illinois, and Tucson, Arizona.

Made in the
USA
Columbia, SC